Magic

Academy

Book 2

Murder At Seagrove

by E.R. Ross

Superstorm Productions, LLC

Other Works by E.R. Ross:

Magic Academy Series

Book One: **The Fire Test**

Book Two: **Murder at Seagrove**

Coming Soon:

Book Three: **Race to Red Skull**

Cover Design by Phatpuppy Art
Cover logo/font by Eden Crane

First American Edition Published in 2015 by Superstorm Productions,
LLC
ISBN 978-1-941994-20-7

Magic Academy Book 2: Murder At Seagrove
2015 Copyright by Superstorm Productions, LLC

Website address: superstormproductions.wordpress.com
Rights & requests & fan mail & hate mail & "meh" mail:
superstormproductions@gmail.com

Many thanks to those who stand against the darkness,

in big ways and small.

Grip fast.

Chapter One
Cloud Temple

Lace Labrencias looked in wonder at the sky temple. The walls were made of wispy pink cirrus clouds and the floor shimmered like stardust. Moss grew up the walls, dotted with silver budding flowers, like tiny stars. The room smelled faintly of violets and sugar snap peas.

Six columns lined the middle of the room, etched with beautiful designs. Tall, narrow windows flooded the floor with strips of warm light.

"Your hair looks pink. It's reflecting the light," Raj said, words lilting in his strange accent. He floated right at her side.

Lace smiled. "I've always wanted pink hair."

The first time she'd picked his aura up, he was so nervous she'd been afraid he was going to puke. He tried to hide it, but she could tell that being in the air terrified him. She wondered whether it was the 'not being in control' part of it, or the fact that if she dropped him, he'd be dead.

But slowly, as they flew together more often, he began to relax. Began to trust her. And now he looked as calm as a duck in water. His muscular shoulders were loose, his striking jaw relaxed. His long fingers waded through the air gently, as if he were treading water. And his bright green eyes sharply took in everything around him.

This new ability was Professor Bahir's doing. He taught Lace how to carry and control the aura of others. So far she could only do it with Raj, because they had a strange compatibility, but Bahir had warned her that she'd have to stretch that 'magic muscle' even more today.

Lace had threaded his aura through hers. It'd taken awhile. She'd woven their threads like a basket, meticulously blending them, her silver with his orange, her silver with his orange, until they were stuck fast. It was only the surface of their auras but it was more than she'd done with anyone else.

The attachment set all of her nerves on fire, she'd never been aware of anyone like she was of him—his gold-righteous soul, his deep heart beating, his powerful body moving in perfect time with hers. He was the closest person to her at the academy—but their relationship was also the most complicated. An intoxicating blend of familiarity and mystery.

She couldn't decide if she loved it or hated it.

"We'd better get to work on Professor's assignment," she said.

This was their classroom. Her body was perfectly safe in Professor Bahir's study. Bahir transported the students to this dimension with his mind, a feat very few magicians were capable of.

Every day the students were trained in a different mind palace. Yesterday it had been underwater, the day before in space. They'd had three weeks of school so far. In the mornings they sat in the library as Bahir lectured them about magical theory. In the afternoons they practiced the theories—yesterday they'd practiced levitation spells in a muddy forest in Mount Grimstone, and Lace had ended up face first in a mud puddle. Just perfect. In the evenings they read more magical theory.

It was more magical theory than she could handle.

Lace felt like she was moving backwards rather than forwards in her knowledge. She thought she'd progressed well in her training at home but here discovered she'd only scratched the surface. Whatever she thought she knew, she didn't. Professor Bahir had to reteach everything.

She made mistakes every day. She was failing assignments. Landing in mud puddles. Being laughed at by

Delia and Arif. It was beyond frustrating.

And she could barely grasp the old assignments he gave her before he gave her new ones. Like now.

The students had three objectives on this mission: get an iron box out of the sky temple, do it in less than ten minutes, and stay alive. The box was taller than One Eye and had a few glowing spells on it that Lace couldn't understand. Everyone had circled the iron box, discussing ideas on how to solve the puzzle. Lace and Raj had left to explore the room.

"Fly higher," Raj said.

She shot up. The exhilaration of flight captured her and she ducked and curved around the columns. Raj mirrored her movements, his green eyes shining. Her skirt fluttered around her ankles. Tendrils of hair bounced and waved at the speed.

Unable to hold it back she smiled. Raj smiled and then laughed, as if he couldn't hold back anymore.

"You like flying?" she asked.

"Yes!" he exclaimed. "I don't know why you ever walk."

"I don't if I can help it. Nothing's comparable to the thrill of being the wind!"

"Aye, you two!" Delia shouted from below. She wore a resplendent sage green gown and her hair was curled and done in a stylish twist. Gods, how could she look like she stepped out of a painting at all times? Her aura was bright red, in command mode. "Stop flittering and see if those windows can be opened." The ex-queen was the self-announced leader, grabbing the title as if there was no possible way it could fit anyone else, despite Bahir's warnings against it.

The exhilaration drained from Lace. She looked down at the box with a guilty glance, conscious of the slipping time. She flew up towards the windows.

"Is flittering even a word?" Raj whispered.

Lace spoke in a mocking lofty voice. "It is if the queen *says* it is."

A flicker of a grin lit his eye, then he went serious. "Let's see if we can use these windows."

"We can if the queen *says* we can."

They leveled off at the window. There was no way the box could fit through unless they smashed some of the wall with it too. Lace swiped her fingers through the wall—it was made of gritty pink cloud-goo, it felt like dipping into whipped mortar.

What other options did they have?

She peeked out one of the huge glass windows. They were so far above the earth that the trees were just dots on the landscape and clouds were eye-level. Quite a fall.

They flew back down and landed on the marble floor. Raj stumbled awkwardly and lurched forward, trying to regain his equilibrium.

"Sorry," she said. "Forgot to teach you how to land." Lace held her arms out to her side and slowly lowered, toes first, in a gentle descent.

Delia lifted her arms towards the box, using her magic. There was a loud *crack*, and an explosion of red dust. The box stayed unmoved.

"There is a counter-spell on it," Cannon said.

"Got that," Delia said. "Or Kaina is messing with my powers again."

Cannon shook his head. "If Kaina was messing with your powers you wouldn't have any."

Delia shrugged, conceding.

Raj tried reverse summoning it out the window but nothing happened.

Violet, her frizzy hair tied back with a purple handkerchief, was playing with the moss on the wall. She lifted her hand to it and tendrils of the greenery rose and wrapped around her slender wrist. A bud bloomed to life, unfolding its soft petals as if greeting her. Her aura was white with peace.

Making friends with flora and fauna was her work— time and time again they'd been saved by a tree or animal Violet had manipulated.

Raj, Arif, Cannon, and One Eye tried to heft it up, with

Delia directing them. One Eye was by far the strongest and tallest of them and when he lifted his corner the weight landed opposite him—right to the scrawny young pirate, Arif. From the sounds of their guttural grunts and exclamations it wasn't working too well.

"Oy, stop pushing it my way," Arif snapped. One Eye bent his knees and lowered his side, which gave him an awkward gait. They were barely able to budge it half a length, there was no way they could transport it across the room.

Lace went through all their options, and was beginning to get an idea.

"A little help?" Raj called to her.

"Quit staring and help us out," Delia ordered, with a hard edge to her voice, as usual. The soothing baths Bahir set up for them at the end of the day were obviously not working. "Put it down, men!" Delia said. "You'll only break a leg. We have to figure out how to let magic do the work for us. If only we had a dozen Yellow-Lander men, they'd make quick work of it."

Delia's words struck like a barb—easy for her to say but impossible to pull out of Lace's skin. She often said racist remarks without thinking, and every time Lace burned with anger. She should be stolid and unemotional like her father, but in truth she felt like wrenching Delia's aura out the window. She ignored the comment, for now. Responding to it would only get in the way of their work.

Just as the men released the box, Lace tried something. Because there were so many spells on the box, it glowed with an aura. She grabbed the magic in the iron box's aura. It was too heavy. Grunting, she remembered what Bahir told her. Separate her aura into even tinier threads and her grip would be stronger.

Stretching and separating her aura, she sewed it into the box's aura. Then she gripped it, muscles straining. It slowly rose. She raised it until it was eye-level with the group below, hovering above the ground. Arif's mouth fell open. "You've been holding out on us, Lace."

"How did you—" Cannon started. "That's amazing!"

But it was too heavy. Her arms shook and her magic sank at an alarming rate.

She released the aura and it dropped with a *thud*. The men scooted back, aware of their toes being crushed.

One Eye held up four fingers. Scad. Not much time left.

Violet suddenly turned from the flowers, as if just noticing where they were. "Now how do we get this box out of the room?" she said as she walked to them.

An idea lit. Lace's face brightened. "We don't move the box, we move the room!"

Cannon clenched his fist. "Yes!" His eyes wandered the room, bright with thoughts.

Delia snorted. "I'd rather not fall a thousand feet to my death."

"I don't get how we could—" Raj began, then was interrupted by Arif.

"Why are we in magic school if our damn magic doesn't work?" Arif pounded his fist against the box and thunder rumbled from outside.

"Without other skills, magic means nothing," Raj said.

"*That's* scad," Arif argued. "My magic is everything."

"You're young," Raj said with just a hint of disdain. As if he was so old, when actually he was no more than twenty-two.

One Eye held his hand up high so everyone looked at him, then he pointed at Lace with a questioning look in his eye. Anytime Lace looked at One Eye she became aware of all the superfluous words she used, as he never used *any* but he could communicate so much.

What should they do? He looked to her to direct them.

Lace took a deep breath and held it, thinking. Then she spoke quickly, all in one breath. "Delia, transform some of the floor beneath the box to air or bamboo, to make it weaker. Violet, make a platform from the vines for us to hang on to. Arif, build a strong force of wind under the floor, to sweep it away once it falls. Raj, reverse summon the floor. One Eye, help everyone on the vine platform. And look out for stray demons."

"I don't think that's going to work," Delia said. She folded her arms across her chest.

Lace narrowed her eyes. "Are you saying that because you have a better idea, or because you didn't think of it yourself?"

In reality, she wasn't sure if it would work either. But they were running out of time and had no time for Delia's whine.

As she was speaking, Violet had already gotten to work. She surfed her fingers through the air, twirling and walking on tip-toe as she wove her magic into the vines. A minty fragrance filled the air. Soon, she'd woven a second floor above the box.

Arif pulled his sleeves up, revealing the colorful rune tattoos, and started a form. Bent knees, slow practiced movements, wide arcs of his hand—his aura cleared and focused as he drew in the air, forming and uniting with the weather until he became a force himself. It was beautiful to watch.

He called to the wind until it whistled and whooshed around them.

No matter how many times she was exposed to it . . . damn, magic was fantastic.

They had to wedge between the woven greenery so that

One Eye could lift them on top of the vines. Delia's magic was performed in a second, though Lace noticed how depleted her magic was from the substantial arcane act. The floor had been turned into half wood, half glass—and Delia had even created a design in it. As if they needed something pretty to look at.

Lace took to the air and flew above the vines, hovering over the students as One Eye helped each one to the lush, green perch.

Soon they were all settled on vines that were hopefully strong enough to carry them all.

That was a big hope. Lace would hate to fail in front of everyone. Again.

"Think they'll hold all our weight?" Cannon asked Violet.

"Of course!" Violet said. "Well, I think so. Probably. Um . . . maybe?" She bit her lip and gripped one of the vines, as if willing it to hold fast.

"I really wish I hadn't eaten that extra sausage link for lunch," Cannon laughed. "Gods, wow." Cannon rested his hand on the vines, so intricately woven together in Violet's control. "You have such an incredible gift, how you can create life like this." Violet beamed. "And I'm sure glad you *never* get this rattan vine confused with poisoned teeth vines."

A tendril wrapped around her wrist. "Oh, this is stinging hammer vine," she said, straight faced.

He narrowed his eyes. "You know that its pollen is poisonous when—"

"It's not really," she said with a grin. "Hammer vines have white buds, not silver."

He laughed.

At first Cannon's optimism made Lace think of him as childish or naive—but the more she got to know him the more she realized he was just a very kind man. Also, the most intelligent and academically minded of all the students. Though Cannon was not one for physical feats (he didn't even carry a knife), and his healing magic wasn't too useful during most assignments, he added something invaluable—camaraderie.

One Eye lifted one finger.

"We have got to act *now*," Delia said. "I sure hope your plan works." She shot a look at Lace.

"Catch us if the vines don't hold," Arif told her. "All right?"

Lace nodded. But she absolutely did *not* believe she could not carry this many. It'd be the first time to even attempt it. It'd be like trying to hold up a horse on her own.

One Eye clapped so loud it startled Lace. He made a chopping motion with his hand. Scad. Time's up.

"Arif, prepare the wind. Release the floor on my count, Raj," Lace said. "One. Two." She took a quick breath, preparing to hold everyone's auras lest the vines break. "Three!"

Raj swiped his hands through the air and then three things happened at once: The floor disappeared and the box fell straight down, dropping swiftly, Arif's air currents whipped into the room so sharply that they—along with the students' gathered weight—snapped the vines from their connection with the wall. They dropped. Violet gave a panicked scream.

"Scad!" Lace dove after them. Wind whistled in her ear.

The group tumbled through the air, head over heels.

Lace clenched her muscles and gripped every aura she could find. Straining, searching, reaching for their souls. She pictured each person, one after the other. But Delia's aura was so sharp, then One Eye was too dense, and Violet slipped through and she had no idea where Arif even was. Gods, she was losing them all!

With a jerk, she caught herself midair and watched their figures fade.

Damn. She'd failed again.

She wasn't strong enough. Her face flushed and her breathing came hard, and even though she knew that Professor Bahir would pull the students back home before they landed, at the sight of her friends falling to their deaths before her eyes smarted. When would she learn how to carry them?

There was a noise above her. Someone cleared their throat.

Startled, Lace looked up.

Raj was caught in the aura with her. Sunlight streamed around his figure and his light blue tunic blended into the sky, making his skin appear darker than usual.

"You've swept me off my feet again, Princess Lace," Raj said.

They stared, wind whipping their clothes and hair, and she wanted to say something but didn't know what.

Then everything went black.

Chapter Two
The Bath

When she opened her eyes she was strapped on a table in Bahir's study. Her muscles were stiff. Although the experience was all in her mind, her body still went through the motions.

The study was lit with gas lamps, smelling of smoke and oil. One wall was a bookcase, full to the seams with ancient manuscripts and Professor Bahir's romantic poetry collection. On the other wall was his very rare, extensive collection of ancient masks from the Minnin Period.

The students had already gotten up from their tables and were gathered around Bahir's desk, respectfully waiting on him to finish writing something. Lace tried to ignore Delia's glares.

Kaina came up to her without a word and unbuckled the

straps. She was the oddest among them—two-hundred and eleven years ago the last goddess who lived on earth had split into a dozen pieces and one of them had been embedded in Kaina's little body—she was a seven-year-old demi-goddess. Her aura was incredibly hard to read; Lace couldn't understand most of it. And since the girl goddess barely ever spoke and never reached out to her, Lace couldn't define who she was.

All she knew was that she was good-hearted. Which was all that mattered, really.

Lace stretched and jumped off the table. She eagerly went to Raj's side and started unstrapping him. "Our flight was much smoother than last time."

He didn't meet her eyes. "Still failed." He sat up, rubbing his wrists.

Guilt seared like a brand. If only she was stronger, she could have saved everyone.

They walked to the desk to await their lecture. Would it be on magical theory again? Or would he tell a story from his past to teach them a lesson? Or would he make them break down what had happened? Lace swallowed and shifted from side to side with nervous energy.

Finally, Bahir looked up. He wore a tailored silk jacket and pants, and his long white hair was pulled back in a ponytail. His ears were pierced with gold hoops, and he painted his fingernails black as all traditional Dram Elders did. His kind brown eyes observed them for a moment before he adjusted the book on his desk and said in his old, shaky voice, "What did we learn from that?"

Arif took a deep breath and began, "I shouldn't have gathered the wind with such force."

Violet cleared her throat. "And I should've twined the vines together to make them stronger. Next time I will create them thicker."

"I learned that I should trust my gut—" Delia said, raising her chin. "And we should never have listened to Lace."

The words burned, but Lace just set her jaw. There was no reason to fight back or expect Delia to respect her—it'd be like putting a rock into a pot and expecting it to melt into butter. Although her face warmed from embarrassment, she tried to shove down her ego.

Her goal here was to learn magic, not fight with a spoiled queen.

Lace spoke softly. "I learned that it's much easier to lift things when my aura is split into small braids . . ." she paused, swallowing. "And that I really need to learn how to carry everyone."

Raj stepped forward. His aura was a beautiful, intimate blue. "I want to learn to think outside the box. Like Lace did."

One Eye nodded.

Her face warmed again, but this time it was from pleasure.

Professor Bahir nodded, accepting everyone's words. Looks like they weren't going to get a lecture after all. "For your last assignment of the day I want you to meditate on your gifts, and visualize them outside your own preferences and experiences . . . imagine them outside the box you've put them in."

They bowed low. "Yes, professor," they said.

"Lace." Bahir looked down, marking something on his paper. "I need to speak with you. Students, you may leave."

From the corner of her eye she saw Delia smirk. Lace sighed. Looks like she was the *only* one who deserved to get the lecture on magical theory.

They bowed again, then streamed out of the room.

The clock on the wall ticked loudly, and the flames crackled in the fireplace. Violet had put a hydrangea bush in a pot beside the window, and she could smell the blooms.

Professor Bahir stood and walked around the desk, then sat on it and patted the space next to him. She slowly walked over and sat beside him.

They sat in amiable silence.

He finally spoke. "You know what I want your next goal to be?"

Lace nodded. "I need to learn how to carry more than one person's aura."

"No." He clasped his hands together in his lap. "You need to befriend Delia."

Wait—what? That is the opposite of what she needed to do here. The only way she could survive was to ignore such people. "You're asking too much!" Lace exclaimed, unable to hide the emotions from her voice. "I came to learn magic."

He spoke earnestly. "You know more than everyone here that magic is tied to the soul. Delia's actually the only one who can teach you about how to carry more than one person."

"What? How?" Lace was confused. Delia's magical ability was transfigurations, not reading auras.

"You'll have to ask her," Bahir said pointedly.

Lace winced. She felt as if he'd just asked her to sleep with the cows.

"She's a person," Bahir said.

Lace crossed her arms, frowning.

"She's a hurting person who has never had any friends her whole life, besides Cannon. You're going to teach her how."

She gritted her teeth, not wanting to hear it.

"It's your next assignment," Bahir said heavily. "Indicate that you understand."

Lace gave a quick nod, and then jumped off the desk and stalked out the room. At the door, she felt a twinge of responsibility and turned and bowed before exiting.

Bahir bowed back to her, ever respectful.

If she'd stayed in there a moment longer she would have exploded and splattered anger all over the professor. It wasn't fair of him to ask her to befriend such a woman. Isn't it Delia who should change? Why must Lace walk to Delia, rather than Delia walk to Lace?

It wasn't fair at all.

The tumultuous thoughts filled her so that she didn't even remember the walk to her room. She closed the door and leaned against it.

Finally, alone.

Her introverted spirit had been worn thin these past few weeks. She liked people—but they drained her. At home she'd had long bouts of alone time, either at night when she read until the moon rose high in the sky, or long mornings when she'd patrol the boundaries with her horse.

Her new room was simple and elegant, Professor Bahir was rich and knew how to take care of his students. Soft silk sheets and a smooth cotton blanket, a feather mattress, heavy chest of drawers, in which she kept her other dress (she only owned three), and a bath with a pipe that drained out the wall. The only decoration was a watercolor painting of the sea above her bed, unless you counted the window, which displayed the magnificent Moth Valley.

The bath had been drawn; it was steaming and full of bubbles, courtesy of the household servant. She'd never had a servant before, and it felt strange to have things like that done for her. Although she felt less guilty when she learned that the servant performed most of his tasks through magic.

Still deep in thought, she shed her sandals and peeled out of her dress, draped it over her bed, and then slipped into the warm water.

The soap was lavender scented, and the comfort of it stopped her negative pondering. It felt so good to be suspended in water, surrounded in warmth. She gently ran her hands along her entire body. All the sweat and grime washed away. She leaned against the back of the tub and closed her eyes, letting the void envelop her. Her muscles lost their tension.

Breathe in, breathe out. Breathe in, breathe out. She focused on clearing her mind and meditating on her gifts, as Bahir had instructed. But it was hard to focus—her thoughts kept bouncing from worrying about Delia and what a friendship with her would look like, to wondering what the next assignment would be and if she could handle it . . . to imagining Raj's intense eyes on her.

After realizing that she was just wasting time trying to

meditate when her mind was in a knot, she knew what she needed to do.

Release the knot. Her sexual energies were pent up, which clouded her mind.

Tenderly, she put her finger between her brown legs and stroked, leaning back, lips parted. She lightly played on her clit, like a musical instrument, until it felt like music filled her. The climax came quickly—waves of pleasure rolling over her skin, pulsing through her blood, thrilling her mind. She lay back in the water, panting and flushed, a little smile on her lips. That was always what she needed to clear her mind.

With a happy sigh, she stood up. The water flowed off her and dripped into the tub. She reached for the towel.

An aura appeared, one as familiar to her as her own. Not from the door—from out of nowhere. Right in the room!

The next second Raj materialized out of nowhere.

Chapter Three
The Power Inside

She stood before him, skin bare and slick with water. Instead of feeling vulnerable or shocked, she felt a buzz of hot feelings. 'Modesty is not your strong suit,' her sister had always said. She was strong and athletic, her muscles defined, and had always loved being in her skin. And loved men who loved her skin.

Raj's presence seemed to take up the entire room—his aura was so bright—his figure so tall and broad. It looked as if he'd just gotten out of the bath as well. Water dripped from his dark hair—he only wore a loose pair of thin linen shorts, and she could easily see the outline of what was under them.

She smiled.

At first, pleasure brightened his aura, and then a spear of shame cut through. He gasped, then clenched his eyes shut, "Oh gods, oh gods, oh gods," he said in a panicked voice.

Lace grabbed a towel and covered her front with it.

"How did you—um, what the hell are you doing here, Raj?" She hurriedly stepped from the bath. A sheen of sweat erupted on his forehead.

But her feet were oily and slick from the soap—her foot jerked out from under her on the smooth floor. Her arms flew out to regain her balance and the towel fell. With a soft exclamation she winced, bracing for the fall.

Raj glided forward and caught her by her hips, just as she was about to hit the floor. He circled his hand around her smooth stomach as he lifted her, and at his touch, electricity jolted through her. With one hand he brushed the hair back that had fallen in her face and with the other he placed his hand on the small of her back.

She looked up at him and his aura blossomed and curled into an overwhelming desire. For her. His hand stroked her back, causing an electric thrill. Her breath caught in her throat and she looked at his lips, giving him a slow smile. His gaze roved over her face hungrily.

Everything in her wanted to taste him, to feel his lips on hers. Quietly, as if not wanting to spook him, she whispered, "If you slide that hand a bit lower, then—"

"No," he said in a strangled voice, then stepped back.

His aura clouded again with shame. "I never . . . Lace, oh gods . . . I'm so sorry."

Instantly, she felt cold without his arms around her.

The air chilled her wet skin and bumps erupted on her arms. Trying to gloss over his rejection, she walked to the bed and grabbed the blanket, settling it over her shoulders. "How did you get here?" she asked. "I didn't know you had transportation abilities."

Raj stroked his bristly jaw, not looking into her eyes. "I was meditating, imagining—" he cut himself off, then swallowed. "Trying to expand my abilities and I realized I might be able to reverse summon myself. Then I ended up here."

Lace raised her eyebrows, impressed. "Brilliant. That'll be useful!"

He turned to go, but she didn't want the moment to end. They never got the chance to be alone. "Why don't you just reverse summon yourself into King James' chambers and end this war before it starts? So easy."

Raj stopped at the door. The candlelight reflected glistening light off his dark back, marred with scars from his time of captivity. "That's been tried," he said solemnly. "But there are too many defensive spells on the castle." He glanced back at her, then gave a little gasp. "Gods help me, I've got to leave."

He opened the door.

"Don't go," she said.

He paused.

"Stay with me." She clenched the blanket tighter around her shoulders and said what she'd known since they met: "When we're together, I'm stronger."

He turned to her, expression brimming with emotion. His green eyes were framed with long eyelashes. It looked like something was on the tip of his tongue, but he couldn't say it.

What was it? What was he needing to say?

"You don't need me," finally came from his lips. "You are strong alone. Strong enough to handle anything Bahir gives you, you know?"

She set her jaw and looked down. No, she didn't. Not really. She'd failed at almost everything so far.

"Don't doubt yourself, or listen too much to others," he said. "You've the power already, inside yourself." For a moment she believed him—his aura was true—he believed in her with his whole heart. "You don't need me," he said again, as if pleading with her.

"Well," she said softly. "What if I don't need you?" She sent him a piercing glance. "I just *want* you."

"Gods help me." He groaned.

She leaned forward. "Stay and talk with me!"

His lips parted and he grazed her body with his eyes. "You are altogether too naked . . . we would not be talking."

She chuckled. "Is that so bad?"

"I can't," he whispered.

Then he turned and left, closing the door softly behind him. The dark corners seemed even darker after he'd gone. She took a deep breath and let it all out slowly. The room still smelled of lavender oil.

Raj's desire for her was as obvious as the nicely shaped nose on his face. To see him walk away didn't hurt her feelings—it was a challenge—it lit her up inside. She longed to draw him in somehow.

She slipped on a dress—a flowing, short purple one that had once been her mother's. Then she drained the bathtub, drying out the bubbles so the servant wouldn't have to clean it later. After she blew out the candles only the moon lit her room with silver light.

Curling up on the bed, she wrapped herself like a cocoon with the blanket and lay on the bed.

It felt like she'd just closed her eyes when someone shook her gently awake. The room was dark and everything was quiet. Professor Bahir leaned over her, eyes wide. "I need you, Lace," he said. "There's been a murder!"

Chapter Four
The Seagrove Spy

Sleepiness surrounded her. Her eyelids were heavy and her thoughts dull. She blinked at Professor Bahir, still under her blankets.

Then the news sunk in. She gave a small gasp and sat up. "I'll be right there."

He stalked out the door. Lace quickly slipped out of bed, then paused. She had nothing to wear. Her white dress was still in the laundry, covered in mud, and her pink dress was covered in dirt and green leaf-stains. Looking into the mirror, she wondered if this dress was so bad? It went all the way to her knees, up to her neck . . . but it was very thin.

Through the sheer fabric was the outline of her body, her wide hips, round ass, tights abs, and tits. She'd certainly worn less out, but Professor Bahir seemed pretty formal.

But the other two dresses were in terrible shape—even more embarrassing to wear than showing a little leg.

She'd risk the leg.

After wrapping her soft peach-colored shawl around her shoulders, she hurried out.

In the hallway, she stopped, then spun around and went back into her room. Taking her worn leather belt, she slipped a knife and sheath on it, then buckled it around her waist.

There. She had to stay prepared for anything.

***

Everyone was gathered in the parlor, where big cushions and couches were arranged in a circle around the huge black marble fireplace. Arif had a poker and was stoking the weak fire. The room was still cold and damp—the windows empty black—only the faint glimmer of sunrise on the horizon.

The student's eyes were dim and movements sluggish, weighed by sleepiness. Only One Eye looked fully awake. His eye was bright, his cheeks pink. Delia wore a black corseted dress, intricate red beading swirling down the skirt. Her hair was in a fancy twist around the crown of her head, and her golden curls tumbled down her back. Holy hell. Did she look that good waking up?

Raj didn't meet her eyes, probably still embarrassed about his surprise bath time visit. If he hadn't been so red faced she was going to tease him about it, but she feared he'd melt through the floor.

"We have to hurry," Professor Bahir said behind them, and Lace jumped at his voice, surprised by his sudden appearance in the room. He was dressed for a journey, in a long robe, leather vest, and travel pack. Kaina was at his side, wearing a sweet little pink dress. But her eyes were hard.

"What happened?" Cannon said.

Professor Bahir took off his backpack and handed it to One Eye, who slipped it on. "Our most powerful spy, who is a part of the hierarchy in Seagrove, was murdered tonight." His voice shook and his aura swirled with emotion—Lace had never seen him like this. Whatever had happened shook him up.

"How did you know so fast?" Raj asked.

"Every rebel leader has a spider's web," Bahir said, as if that explained everything rather than clouded it up. His aura ripped a little at the words. "We have to go to Seagrove and discover who did this, and how much of our rebellion they know about." He paled. "Who-who knows what they did to her before they killed her—they-they could know everything."

Lace shivered and stepped closer to the fire, letting its flickering warmth glance off her skin. What if the spy had known about the magic academy? What if their enemies now knew her name? Could her family be in danger?

"Which Hierarch was murdered?" Cannon asked. He and Delia had a good chance of knowing the murdered person, since they lived at the castle for years.

Firelight flickered shadows over them all. Professor Bahir swallowed. "It was Willow Stem."

Cannon gasped. "Willow? Oh no! No!" His face wrinkled in distress. He grabbed Delia's hand and she put an arm around his shoulder.

"I can't believe it," Delia said in shock.

"You know her very well, Professor Bahir?" Lace said, eyes soft, for she already knew the answer.

Bahir hesitated, and a look of pain crossed his features. His aura shadowed with sadness—no, more than that. Grief. "She was my wife."

Everyone froze.

Violet turned to him. "I didn't know you were married."

"*Was* married." Bahir sighed so heavily it sounded like the weight of the world was on his shoulders.

Bahir shifted and glanced at everyone nervously. "We can't—can't talk about this now, we have to get there before the Centurions do."

"But," Lace protested. "We need the back story if we're going to be any help solving the murder."

The professor stared at her hard, as if searching her intentions. Then he conceded. "When I was high chief mage at King James' castle the only person I really knew was Willow. She was the daughter of a new and tenuous Hierarch in the land—she was thirsty for my knowledge of the culture and I was thirsty for her knowledge of politics. We helped each other out, and worked well as a team. So we were married with King James' blessing."

From the way he talked about it, she wasn't sure he was entirely in love with Willow. Or if he had been, it had long died out. It sounded like more of an agreeable match than a passionate love affair. A lover should be spoken of with longing and joy and need.

"The more we saw of King James' practices and the more greedy and evil he became, the more we were of one mind about something: he must be stopped. It was on the eve that he built the Hexagon that we swore we would give our lives to defeating him."

"You knew it that early on?" Raj asked, surprised. "Why did you stay with him?"

Professor Bahir formed a tent with his fingers and he frowned deeply. "There was a great debate between myself and my wife about the method in which we should take him down. You see, Willow wanted to work from within the system—she wanted to be involved in the laws and the leadership and bear as much burden for the people as she could. But me, I wanted to leave right away and destroy him from the outside." He sighed. "Our disagreement was so deep that we couldn't stay together anymore. She divorced me and married Stim, becoming Hierarch of Seagrove. I escaped the court and we never saw each other again."

"But she's been helping you," Lace said.

He nodded. "Every new moon she sends me a message with information regarding King James' plans. What she's given me has been invaluable to our cause—it's convinced me that we can't just have people outside, we have to have them inside as well if we want to take down this evil. She was right after all."

"But she had to make some serious compromises, to be a hierarch," Lace said.

That must have struck a chord in Cannon. He spoke up, blue eyes flashing. "In order to defeat evil we all do as much as we can. That's what I've learned. Willow did it from the inside, we are doing it from outside. We don't just need warriors and politicians to help defeat this ruthless kingdom. Whether it's a slave passing on a bit of information or a farmer giving food to hungry children or a king building a wall to protect his land, we do what's in our power. We can't do anything more."

"It takes all kinds," Bahir said.

"And now she's gone," Delia said. "Is there anyone to replace her?"

"No," Professor Bahir said. "Our rebellion lost an important ally."

"If a hierarch was murdered . . ." Violet began, speaking slowly.

Arif poked the fire one last time then turned around. "Then King James' Centurions will be there to punish the murderer. Maybe even punish the town. In the past, King James has burned entire villages because they treated tax collectors disrespectfully. This is severe."

"Is everyone armed?" Bahir said.

Arif gripped the handle of his sword and Raj checked his throwing knives. Lace wondered if Delia had a crossbow in that huge skirt of hers?

Violet shook her hands in the air. "These arms are all I need."

"Stand in a circle, everyone," Bahir ordered.

Lace was still heavy with sleep and processing all she had heard. Sometimes it took her awhile to adjust to things, to find a place for it in her mind.

Raj stood beside her. Close. Without even thinking, as if the action was natural as breath, she took his hand and slipped his fingers through hers. He paused, holding his breath, then slowly slipped his hand out of hers.

"Our assignment is to impersonate the Centurions," Bahir said. "And discover who the murderer is and what they know. All before the real Centurions get there."

They couldn't possibly be ready to fight the Centurions yet. She felt overwhelmed by the task—how could she be of any use on such an important mission? The Centurions were the best mages in the whole country. Possibly the whole world.

One Eye's eyebrows raised.

"How much time do we have?" Raj asked.

"If the King already knows about it, it'll still take them four hours to fly to Seagrove," Kaina said in her high, weird voice. "Unless there's a factor we don't know about. Like they take the magnetic trail."

Magnetic trails were the only way to travel through a portal—they coiled around the earth like invisible rivers— only certain mages were able to find them. She'd learned that in class last week.

"Then let's leave now," Bahir said in a grim tone. "Kaina will stay behind and protect the castle."

The girl stepped back until she blended into the dark shadows at the doorway. She was strange.

They crowded close. Entranced, Lace saw how their auras wove and knit together in a braid that stretched from shoulder to shoulder. They were connected, whether they recognized it or not. It was a good sign.

Professor Bahir completely relaxed, closed his eyes and

breathed out a low, guttural sound.

"Wait!" Delia suddenly shouted. She was staring at Lace, horrified. Bahir's eyes flew open and everyone tensed, looking around. "Oh gods, Lace! You can't go to Seagrove wearing that. They'll mistake you for a whore!"

Chapter Five
The Dress

Everyone stared at the short purple dress, scrutinizing, ogling . . . and she wished it was some dream she'd wake up from.

Her chest tightened and a wave of shame reeled over her, though she told herself she had nothing to be ashamed of. At that, a deep knot of rage gutted her.

It was Raj who jumped in front and barred her from Delia, as if the queen were about to physically attack. "Don't speak to Lace that way." His voice shivered in anger.

Professor Bahir's voice was shocked. "My dear, how could you?"

Lace's head jerked up—was he speaking to her? But no—he stared wide-eyed at Delia, as did everyone else.

Delia swallowed, suddenly hesitant. "W-w-well it was

the truth."

"My ass it was," Arif said. "I praised the gods when I saw Lace in that dress."

Professor Bahir took a few breaths before responding, and everything seemed to still. "The truth, my dear Delia, must be covered in kindness and peace, or it is like rubbing scad all over a flower then giving it to Lace." He put his palms together as a sign of respect, and Lace leaned forward, intent on what he would say next. "Lace, I'm sorry, but it is true that you must change."

Lace snorted, her shoulders grew so tense they knotted in pain. The anger was growing, creating a sheen over everything. "I wear less than this at royal meetings with—"

Bahir snapped his finger, interrupting her. "It's true for Zoto. But Seagrove is a conservative town and you'd have the leaders in distress if they saw you."

Gods, this was scad. But not a fight for today. "I'll change. This doesn't have a belt for my sword, anyway . . ."

She felt like throwing a fit—burning Delia with her words—but instead, she clenched her fists and grabbed the air's aura with all her might and shot out of the room, flying so fast her feet flew sideways behind her, swerving so she narrowly missed crashing into the hallway. By the time she reached her doorway she was panting.

She went in and slammed the door shut, then stopped.

What would her father think of such antics?

That thought froze her. He'd always said, "Whether people respect you or not doesn't matter, you can't control them. What you can control is respecting yourself."

Then she shoved that thought away, for the pain and embarrassment of Delia's words were still too sharp, too raw. She wrenched out of her dress, shoved it in the drawer, and wriggled into her chemise and dirty dress.

Each button seemed to take forever, and she fumed about keeping all the team waiting as she did something as banal as changing clothes. When she buttoned the last two she slipped on her sandals and grabbed her shawl and went out the door.

No, wait.

She unbuttoned the top buttons until it showed a shadow of cleavage. They could make her change, but she was going to keep a little rebellion.

Chapter Six
First Battle

Lace flew back into the room, then jerked the air's aura so suddenly to stop that a gust of air blew everyone back a step and doused the fire. The release of power had felt good. Almost as good as screaming into a pillow.

"Let's go," she said in a hard voice.

Violet gave her a wink.

They reformed their circle and Professor Bahir began his spell.

Raj didn't take up her hand, as if sensing the waters were tentative around her. But standing beside him, a feeling of protection held her. He was a strong ally.

She stilled, preparing herself. Magnetic trail portals were never comfortable. They were deep magic, and rare. She doubted that anyone else in all of the land could transport eight people hundreds of miles through a portal, besides Bahir.

There was a gut-wrenching tug on her stomach—as if someone had grabbed her insides. She grimaced, and held back a groan. Then her skin tingled all over, like cold fire danced on it.

Professor Bahir said a word, "*Jinti*," and then it was like her whole being was sucked through the space of a coin. Everything warped and squeezed together. Her stomach jolted. She closed her eyes and swallowed back the bile.

Throwing up in a portal would be horrible. Delia would probably never let her hear the end of it.

With a *hurk*, they were transported.

Everything grew back to size, twisting and popping and bulging, and Lace felt all her pieces expand back in place. It was not exactly painful, it was more like cracking a stiff joint—a hint of pain but more relief than not. She leaned over, panting and squinting her eyes shut, trying to become herself again. The roaring in her ears subsided.

Then it was quiet.

She felt stone under her feet and a breeze on her neck.

Opening her eyes, she saw they were in an abandoned temple ruin. Arches without roofs towered above them in a perfect circle. They stood on a faded ancient mosaic. So this was where the magnetic road led to. On the horizon was the sea—vast, white foamed, and angry. Nestled beside it was a small town.

The sun was just peeping up over the horizon. Dawn had come.

In a moment, she took all that in.

The next second she realized that they were completely surrounded by Centurions, King James' mages. They were armed. Zoned in. Ready for battle.

"Run!" Professor Bahir shouted in a strangled voice.

On a reflex, Lace grabbed Raj's aura and shot straight into the air, like an arrow. He cried out. Wind rustled in her ears and she didn't look to the side, only flew as fast as she could, gripping handful after handful of the air's aura.

She heard an explosion under them.

"Stop!" Raj said.

Twisting around, she closed off her vision and only spied auras. It helped her concentrate. Glowing souls moved around the ground, and some flew in the air. She took stock as quickly as she could, assessing and studying them. Taking a deep breath, she yelled as loud as she could, "There are six Centurions! Two spellcasters, two naturalists, a summoner, and a changer."

The summoner suddenly disappeared and appeared again—right behind One Eye.

"One Eye!" Lace screamed. "Look out!"

The huge man leapt back just as the summoner's sword came down—narrowly missing One Eye's neck.

"We have to go back," Raj said. His aura glowed with pent up magic. For a second she was overcome with panic at the thought of facing the King's guards—she wanted to fly away with Raj, to leave, to hide, to never come back. This was too much. She was too young. Too inexperienced. Too weak, she couldn't even—

"We have to go back," Raj said softly. He touched her arm, firm and yearning. His aura wrapped around hers and stuck fast—strengthening, bolstering her own.

The fear that gripped her so tightly succumbed, and at the thought of people in peril the choice became simple.

Save them.

Lace flipped over and dove. The speed made the wind whistle in her ears. She wove to and fro so they were moving targets. Raj's hands glowed orange as he worked his magic.

One Eye was in a tight sword fight with the summoner— who kept trying to use magic on One Eye's sword but it wouldn't budge because Raj had applied a counter curse to it. They were locked in a fierce duel, one just as quick as the other, parrying, attacking. Wait, no . . . it was less refined. More like hacking, grunting. And then more hacking.

Arif was trapped by a golden force field. He pounded on it to no avail, eyes wide and panicked.

Identical twin spellcasters, who both had long white-blonde hair, translucent ivory skin, and small blue eyes, had surrounded Bahir and they shot spells back and forth—fiery pink lightning and glowing green fireballs and eerie white mist. The professor's hair had gone wild and his robes were torn. Blood dripped out the corner of his mouth and there was a gash on his forehead.

Delia transformed one of the arches into a wall, protecting Cannon. Her whole being glowed pink as magic poured out of her. A black-haired, black-eyed woman shifted the grass under One Eye's feet into snakes. With a surge of power, Delia transformed it back.

"Look!" Raj pointed.

The two naturalists had trapped Violet. It was a man and woman, completely naked except for loin cloths and gloves with fierce claws. They'd trapped her in the middle of a crystal, which was growing around her body, crushing her. She was twining brambles around their legs, which they disregarded. Her face was red and panicked; she was in dire need.

Lace flew straight for them.

Raj summoned the crystal from around Violet and it disappeared. She gasped for air. The naturalists looked up at them, then lifted into the air.

Gods, they could fly!

Coming straight at her, side by side, they bared their claws. She had to make a choice. "Attack or run?" she asked Raj.

"Let's take them," he said, drawing his sword. She unsheathed her knife.

They clashed—the woman swiped at Lace. The man dove, his claws bared, at Raj. Lace ducked and feigned a left punch then thrust her knife at the woman's stomach. The woman slid sideways, out of reach. Then she twisted over Lace in a breathtaking flip and raked her claws down Lace's back.

Pain burned, white and hot. She cried out and dropped the air's aura, moving to safety and bringing Raj with her.

He'd fared no better. Bloody marks marred his chest, tearing his shirt. And there was a fresh bruise swelling on his cheek.

"Let me down," he said angrily. "I can't fight up here."

The naturalists followed them, quick as light. With a snarl, the woman hacked at Lace like a wild animal, the whites of her eyes showing through her gnarled dreadlocks. Lace blocked the first blow with her forearm, but the second pierced her neck, tearing skin. Warm blood trickled down her back. Lace leaned back and kicked. Her foot met the woman's chest, shoving her back.

Concentrating on not dropping Raj, she lowered him to

the ground then released his aura. As she did, the woman recovered and slashed—Lace blocked it with her knife, then twisted the blade. One of the claws sliced off.

Just as she did that a huge floating column suddenly crashed into the woman. *Wham.* She was knocked down like a fly and landed, limp, on the ground.

Who—?

Raj wielded the gigantic column, summoning it from side to side. He pulled it towards Bahir until it hovered over one of the spellcasters. The naturalist man dove for Raj, sending a powerful force of magic at him. Rocks erupted around Raj's legs and he almost lost control of the column.

It also provided Lace a perfect shot, while the naturalist was distracted.

She pulled her knife back and threw. It sailed, blade over grip, and sunk into the naturalist's bare back. It struck true. His arms convulsed and he fell from the air, landing at Raj's feet.

Raj looked up at her and nodded. Then he maneuvered the column over the spellcaster—and just as the man dodged, Raj jerked it at the last minute and dropped the column. It crushed his legs and he screamed in pain.

Lace rose higher and surveyed the battle.

Violet had completely surrounded the other spellcaster with poison luke. His skin blistered and his muscles clenched in paralysis, giving Bahir enough time to free Arif from his containment.

Arif jumped behind a column, out of sight of the Centurions. What the hell was he doing? He never ran from a fight.

Clouds started roiling in the sky, spinning like boiling water. Wind gusts whipped about, jerking her off balance. A sudden downward gust plowed into her and she grunted from the strain of trying to keep in the air.

She better get out of the way of Arif's magic.

Delia ran to One Eye's defense. She transformed the Centurion's sword into a long loaf of bread. One Eye punched the man in the mouth—he fell to the ground, holding a bloody jaw. But a second later, the Centurion changer had transformed his sword back. This time it had a hook on the end of it. One Eye lunged with his sword straight for the man's heart but he rolled. One Eye hit the ground.

Raj summoned a net, still wet from the sea, and threw it over the changer's body. She instantly transformed it into an explosion of feathers, which floated around the scene like big snowflakes. The man punched One Eye across the face and then plunged a knife in his shoulder. The big man tensed in pain, then backhanded the attacker away.

Blood soaked through One Eye's shirt.

Battle rage overcame Lace and it felt like there was a

smoldering coal in place of her heart. These bastards were going to pay.

She dove straight for One Eye's attacker, swooping down behind him. Holding herself back to a complete stop, she swung her legs forward and kicked the man in the back with both feet. It caught him totally off guard.

He went flying. He landed on his chest and smashed into the rock. One Eye kicked him in the side of the face, and he went limp.

One Eye nodded to her, pressing his hand against his wound.

Lace landed, panting, looking around for the next fight. The spellcaster was fully entangled in Violet's poison luke, his body shutting down with paralysis from the sap.

But where was the changer? She'd suddenly disappeared. Even her aura was gone.

"Watch out!" she cried. "The changer has disa—" The changer appeared right behind Raj.

No!

Black mist enveloped the woman and a dark magic overcame her so only her skeleton flashed on and off. Then she raised a shadow-dagger, dripping with poison, about to plunge it into Raj's neck.

Her heart wrenched, squeezed into nothing, and her veins filled with ice. Not Raj. Please, not Raj.

The changer's eyes flashed and she bared her teeth.

Lace grabbed Raj's aura and jerked him forward, out of reach. The woman's knife struck nothing but air. Then Arif stepped from behind the column, glowing with magic.

A loud crack erupted in the sky and a terrible bright light ripped through the air. The lightning clashed the changer. Her body convulsed. Raj was so close he was thrown back and smashed into a crumbled wall.

The changer's hair singed and there were black holes where her eyes used to be. Smoke wafted from her. Her aura went weak, but she was still alive.

Lace double counted the auras—then counted them again, just to make sure. The Centurions were down.

Lace collapsed to her knees, so relieved and stressed that she could barely move. If Raj had been killed, she . . . she . . . she couldn't even think of it.

One Eye shadowed her, pressing on his wound with his handkerchief. Blood poured out his nose, and his eye was swelling shut and growing purple.

It's awful nice that they had a healer in their group. He'll be sorely needed. Though Cannon wasn't the one they turned to in a fight—he was the one they turned to after it, and she was immensely thankful for him.

Delia and Cannon came out from where they were hiding behind the columns and walls, sweaty and disheveled.

The battle wasn't over yet, though. It didn't look like any of the Centurions had been killed. They might wake up at any moment.

Once the rush of battle began to dissipate and she caught her breath, the magnitude of what had just happened ripped through her. She bent, resting her hands on her knees. "How the hell did they know we were coming?" she said.

"Is there a spy?" Arif said angrily.

"An impostor?" Delia said.

Violet's whole body was trembling. "We were completely surrounded, damn, that-that-that was awful."

Professor Bahir looked around, checking on everyone. They'd all survived with all their limbs attached, though One Eye's wound looked painful. "We beat them. Well done, students." His face was pale and his legs trembled. "They had no spy or impostor," he said firmly. "We arrived at exactly the same time as they did—they're on their way to investigate the murder. Now we shall take their place."

"But what if more come through?" Lace asked. She eyed Bahir warily—he wasn't looking very well, and his aura seemed weak.

"I'll put a spell on it that blocks anyone else from coming through," the professor said. He took a shaky step forward, and then he collapsed.

Chapter Seven
The Brand

"Professor!" Lace cried. She'd never seen his aura like this—his magic was thin, spider webbed with holes, instead of thick as a wall. He barely had any arcane energy left.

They all surrounded him and Delia brought out a small cask, holding it to his lips. He took a sip, then spewed it out.

"What was that?" Lace asked, worried.

Delia cleared her throat. "Uh . . . rice wine."

Cannon pressed his hands on Bahir's neck, eyebrows creased in worry. His aura lit up with teal green, deep healing. But before he could use it, Bahir rose up. "No," he whispered weakly. "Don't heal me. Not yet. Heal One Eye."

"Don't be ridiculous, I can heal both of you," Cannon said, but hesitated.

Bahir struggled to sit up, moving Cannon's hand out of

the way and shoved it towards One Eye. With a snap, Cannon sent a healing burst at One Eye—it sunk into the big man's wound like mist back into the earth.

One Eye gave a sigh of relief.

A cooling wind wafted from the sea, bringing with it the smell of brine and fish and seaweed. It tickled the hairs on Lace's neck and cooled her cheeks.

"I can't believe we defeated six Centurions," Violet said, awe in her voice.

"Those weren't Centurions," Cannon said, getting up and nudging one of the pale twins with his toe.

"They are the Centurion's apprentices," Delia said.

A wave of fear washed over Lace. If it was this hard to defeat six Centurions, even when the guards were outnumbered, her heart sunk at the thought of facing the real ones.

Professor Bahir slowly got to his feet, grimacing in pain. Respectful, the students all waited for their orders until he'd straightened and opened his eyes.

"Change of plans," he said, then he gave a set of strange instructions. "One Eye, Arif, drag the Centurions in a line in front of me. Be careful around them. Delia, undress them all." She wrinkled her nose in disgust. "Raj, summon a royal insignia brand from King James' castle. Violet, start a fire. Cannon, find us some water. Lace, scout a one-mile perimeter and make sure no one's approaching. Stay low, don't draw undo attention."

Lace gave a quick nod. "And if there's someone? Should I capture—"

"No, just report back."

She felt Raj's eyes on her as she took off. If only they had a moment together, she'd ask him if he was—shut it. No time for that.

What she should be worrying about was if these Centurions were the scouts, and the real ones would follow.

There were four roads leading to the city. Docks were full of fishing boats, gently rocking in the waves like babies in a cradle. The city was surrounded by a gorgeous, cultivated vineyard to one side, and a fruit orchard on the other. She smelled the fragrant blooms from where she was. Come fall, this would be the most delicious place to stay. Grape juice, grape salad, grape custard . . . Lace loved all things grape.

She followed the small road that led to the city, zooming as quickly as she could. Without even realizing it, she was going faster and using less magic than she ever had before. All those practice sessions and magical theory with Professor Bahir were working.

It had been hard for her to notice on a day-to-day basis whether she'd grown or not during her stay at Magic

Academy. But as she cut through the air she realized that she was better and stronger than when she first arrived, even if she had failed most of her assignments. That gave her a surge of pride.

She flew about a mile out, then curved and started circling around the camp. There were a few farms that she dodged, a herd of goats with a young goatherd that she skirted, and a pack of wolves. When she saw them, she swooped down and touched one on the tail, just for the thrill of it.

There was a sheen of dew over everything. The water sparkled like gems on the grass. Early morning chill clung to the earth, making her cold.

Nothing more interesting than trees and fields was met on the perimeter check, which relieved her. The students were in no shape for another battle. Most of the others' magic had waned. She hoped that Cannon had healed Professor Bahir already.

She sped into the ruins so fast that everyone startled. One Eye drew his sword. Delia gave a little yelp, and Lace held back a grin. "Just me," she said as she landed smoothly.

The Centurion apprentices were lined in a row, their clothes stripped off and folded at their feet. There was a roaring fire, and a branding iron stuck out of it. That was when she noticed that all the Centurions were branded on the side of their neck with the King's insignia. One Eye had that same mark.

Professor Bahir looked even more tired and magic-worn than he was when she'd left. But his health had been restored, and his cheeks were flushed. What kind of magic had he been doing?

He met her eyes with a questioning glance.

"No one there," she said. "Except a few young goatherds . . . I think One Eye could take 'em blindfolded and one handed if they attacked." She winked at him. He winked back. Or, more like blinked with purpose. Because he only had one eye.

"Good, thank you, Lace," Bahir said.

She gathered around the fire. The slashes from the naturalist burned with pain, but she could handle it.

They were all intent on what was coming next. What with the stripped Centurions, the branding iron, and the ticking clock, she had a dreadful feeling about what Bahir was going to say.

"This is the new plan. I've already blocked the magnetic trail so the Centurions can't get through. We are going to impersonate these apprentices," the professor said. "I've locked their minds in a void, and One Eye will stay here and guard the bodies."

For a brief instant Lace felt sorry for the Centurions,

being locked in a void was the most terrifying experience she'd ever had. Time and control of your body was lost, but you were awake for the whole thing.

Then she remembered that they worked for King James and had done heinous deeds in his name. And she didn't feel so bad for them.

"The void spell used the absolute last of my magic. I'll be useless for the next eight hours and you'll have to protect me as you would a child." Bahir didn't look at them, he looked into the fire. "Of course, in order to impersonate them, you must be branded."

Violet gasped. Raj looked from Bahir to Lace, alarmed.

"And that's where Cannon comes in. He'll instantly heal you, so it will cause you the least amount of pain."

"Why didn't you get a brand, Violet?" Arif asked.

She looked down and her shoulders shrunk. "The girls can't be damaged. On the outside."

The prospect of getting burned unhinged Lace, but not as much as the thought of being branded with King James' insignia. No matter how painful the physical pain was, it wasn't as bad as being considered King James' property. Everyone who saw her would associate all her works with him and his mark would be on her forever.

"It seems contradictory—" Lace said, "that we have to become one of King James' servants in order to fight him."

"There is a lot about life that is contradictory," Professor Bahir said.

Arif touched his neck. "My pretty skin will be marred."

Lace wasn't sure if he was joking or not, considering all the colorful tattoos up and down his arms. "Just consider it a new tattoo," she said.

"Ugliest one in the world," he said bitterly.

Bahir continued. "We'll dress as the apprentices and go to town to solve the murder."

"How long do we have?" Delia asked, voice urgent.

"It will take at least five hours for the Centurions to fly from the capital," Bahir said.

"We don't have long." Bahir lifted up the brand. "Who's first?"

Everyone's face curled up in distaste. Arif and Violet stepped back. It surprised Lace when Delia walked forward. "Let me." She pulled up her hair and yanked down the collar on her shirt, then bent to one knee. "Do it quick."

Gods, this was really going to happen.

Cannon slipped his hand in hers and knelt with her. He nodded at Bahir. The professor limped over with the bright, hot brand. Delia's eyes clenched shut. Lace started sweating, just watching it. Magic glowed in the air around Cannon.

With a hiss of melted skin, Bahir pressed the glowing metal to her neck for a second and then quickly jerked it back. Her body tightened in pain.

Then she relaxed. Almost before Bahir lifted the brand her skin went from an agonizing red to a whitish-pink scar. She paused for a second, as if assessing the damage. Then she sniffed and got up. "Just a moment of pain, then it's gone," she said. "Like getting your ears pierced. Cannon is good. Who's next?"

One Eye put his arm around Violet protectively. She looked at the scene with wide eyes, pale face.

Raj kneeled. "My turn."

At the thought of him going through so much pain, Lace looked away. There was a terrible hiss, the smell of burnt flesh, and then it was over. He hadn't made a sound. When she looked, his black skin was marred by a white scar with the evil insignia.

With concern, she noted how far Cannon's magic had receded with just two healings.

Raj touched his new scar, then stood up. He walked over to Lace and stood beside her. A flicker of a frown crossed her expression.

"That sign doesn't become you," she indicated it.

He tenderly touched the pink skin, eyebrows creased. "King James *salted* a town I lived in—my owner turned our auras invisible and hid me in a well as the Centurions wreaked their havoc on everyone. He left his flags around the decimated place—" He grimaced at the memory. "That was the moment I knew I wanted to take them down." He snorted. "Now I am one."

"We do what we must," Arif said and kneeled in front of Bahir. "Time to earn your keep, healer."

Wiping the sweat off his brow, Cannon took a deep breath. "I'm not only healing the wound, I'm cutting out the pain, and regenerating scar tissue."

Arif took his hand. "Let's do it."

Violet was completely pale. She watched wide-eyed while her breath came in sharp gasps.

Scad. Cannon's magic was getting very low. Lace doubted whether he had enough for them all.

After Cannon was branded, Bahir handed the glowing stick to Raj. "You need to brand me," he said, and reached for Cannon's hand. The healer was panting now and Lace could see in his face the worry that he didn't have enough magic for everyone.

Raj gently put his hand on the old man's neck, for support. Then, after a quick glance at Cannon to make ready, he quickly pressed the brand to the neck so fast Lace barely saw it touch. The old man trembled all over and she leapt forward to take his arm, afraid he'd collapse. He stood up. "No, no, I'm fine." He took a trembling breath. "Well done, Cannon."

Now everyone was branded except for Violet and Lace. And Cannon was almost completely out of magic. His aura changed colors as his stress mounted.

"What is it?" Delia asked, sensitive to his worry.

He just shook his head.

Lace set her jaw. If anyone was going to have to go through receiving a brand, then she would take it instead of Violet. That lady had seen more than enough pain during her time as a sex slave.

"Violet," Lace said lightly. "You go next. Hide your face in One Eye's shirt and it'll be over before you know it."

Raj gave her a funny expression, and Delia said in a snide tone, "How kind to let everyone else go before you."

Lace ignored her.

"Will you do it?" Bahir asked Raj. "Your hands are quick."

"*My* hands are quick." Arif stood up straight.

"His hands are gentle," Bahir said.

"Oh," Arif looked down. "As a captain, I'm used to wrestling octopus not braiding daisy chains like the monk."

"I'll do it," Raj said, then glanced at Arif. "Then I'll braid you a daisy chain if you wish."

Arif snorted.

Raj lightly held the brand. If she couldn't see his aura she couldn't see how his emotions flared with nervousness.

But his face was still, his strong jaw set, his eyes accepting to the point of blandness. It made her long to make him show what he was feeling. To show anything.

Violet hid her face in One Eye's shirt, and he seemed as tense and agitated as she was. He looked away when Raj approached with the glowing brand. "It'll be over soon," Raj said. Violet trembled violently. Cannon put his hand on the back of her head and closed his eyes, full of concentration.

Raj performed the branding. Quickly.

All of Cannon's magic drained out at the healing. He shot a harrowed look at Lace, and she understood. She'd have to take it on her own.

Violet's eyes were wet with tears, but she had a crooked grin on her face. "Wasn't as bad as I expected," she said with a laugh, then squeezed One Eye tight. "Doesn't hurt a smidge now." He smiled and hugged her back.

Cannon dropped to his knees. "I-I-I'm so sorry," he said in a wrenched voice.

"I'll fare." Lace stepped up and kneeled before Raj.

Cannon looked up sharply. "You knew? How did you—"

"I can see magic ability through the auras," Lace explained, then leaned her head to the side, exposing her neck. Her heart raced in anticipation of the pain.

"What is it?" Professor Bahir said to Cannon.

He shook his head. His golden hair fell in his eyes and sweat dropped off his chin. "I'm drained."

"Gods, Cannon!" Arif said in an anguished tone. "Why'd you leave Lace for last?"

Raj turned to Bahir. "Let her wear a scarf around her neck. Please, just—"

"No!" Lace said sternly. "We must be thorough. Now hurry and get it over with."

Professor Bahir set his jaw and froze, his eyes bright in thought. Raj leaned forward, as if proximity would bend the verdict. Bahir pressed his hands together in front of his chest and bowed deeply to Lace. "You honor us," he said. Then he snatched the brand out of Raj's hands and set it on her neck.

Chapter Eight
Wild One

Her blood boiled in pain. A scream tore through her lips as her skin melted under the glowing brand. Bahir yanked it away and skin ripped with it. Her scream cut off. She clenched her fists so hard her nails pierced her palms.

A low groan wrenched out of her.

Everything swam and she crouched, resting her hands on her knees. Bile rose in her throat. *Do not faint. Do not faint. Do not faint.*

Trembling all over, she tried to gain some semblance of control. But the pain only increased as the burn sunk deeper and deeper into her skin. It was all she could *feel.* She took steadying breaths, trying to concentrate her world on the next breath. But even breathing hurt.

Cannon groaned. "Oh Lace, I'm so sorry." With shaking

hands, he took out a water cask from his pack and came up to her. "I need to pour this over your burn so the swelling will go down."

She grit her teeth. He gently tilted her head to the side and poured the water directly on the gnarled flesh. At the pressure, she hissed in pain.

But as the cool water flowed, and the burning sensation subsided, it gave her relief. It trickled down her neckline and down her back, dripping onto the grass. Her shoulders relaxed.

"We should go," Delia said.

She couldn't even stand, much less walk right now. How could she be expected to—

"Be quiet, Delia" Bahir said softly.

After a moment, Lace looked up, still frowning heavily from the pain.

Raj was gone. She glanced around and then her face fell when she saw him. He was on the other side of the Centurion's column, panting as if he'd run there. His eyes were on anything other than her, and he was in pain somehow.

The rest of the group, except for Delia, looked at her with profound expressions. "Did you know Cannon was running out of magic?" Arif asked.

The throbbing in her neck had still not dissipated and

she leaned back, unsteady. The ground shifted below her and her head spun.

Professor Bahir threw the brand in the fire. Embers and sparks exploded out of it. "What did we learn from this, students?"

"That Lace is one *tough bitch*," Arif said.

"That I need to strengthen my magic," Cannon said, shamefaced.

"Lace, you waited for last on purpose?" Raj said from across the courtyard.

Lace nodded.

"Noble," he said quietly, though the wind caught it and brought it to her.

"No, no, no," Delia said. "What we need to learn is that the moment we rely on our magic it could get taken away."

"Yes," Bahir said. "Good."

Violet knelt before Lace and kissed her on the forehead. Lace smiled weakly through the pain. "You're a wild one," Violet said as she got up.

Chapter Nine
Disguises

Lace's neck throbbed. The skin blistered and swelled. It was an angry red, and every time she moved even slightly there was searing pain. She'd never had such a wound before. Easing into a cross-legged position, she tried to steady her shaking. If only she had something to—

Raj came quickly to her side, as if reading her mind. He bent a knee beside her and placed his hand on the small of her back, gently easing her down. She relaxed into his side, leaning on his chest, thankful for his strength. His aura was tinged in orange, alarmed and upset. When she looked into the sky and saw their auras, his was even stormier than hers.

It was as if he felt her pain.

The sun began to dry the humidity in the air and warmed her cheeks. The gorgeous tinge of orange on the horizon faded as the sun rose. Birds chirped and in the distance she heard the goats bleating.

Raj asked Cannon, "How long before your magic is—"

"Not too long," Cannon said. "Less than an hour before I have enough to heal her burn."

"I can bear it for an hour," Lace said. She had to.

She reached for the water and Cannon handed it to her. She took a long drink, gulping it down. It was cool and sweet, a balm to her parched throat. From the corner of her vision she felt Raj eyeing her with concern. He was so close she felt his breath on her cheek.

"Between Lace's weakness and Professor Bahir with zero magic, it'll take us hours to make it to Seagrove," Delia said with a sigh.

"I can fly," Lace said in a soft but firm voice, wiping her mouth and handing the water back to Cannon. Too bad she couldn't carry Bahir as well. He looked older than he ever had before.

If only she possessed the ability to carry anyone in the air she wished, but she hadn't learned that yet.

"Everyone get busy putting on the Centurions' clothes," Bahir ordered.

But Raj didn't move. Of which she was glad. She put a hand on his leg and closed her eyes for a second, using him as a support. His aura stilled, as did hers, as if they mirrored each other. She felt the beat of his heart and the scent of his skin and the hard reality of who he was. Someone to lean on.

Well, moving wasn't going to get any less painful.

Though her neck was still hot and throbbing, the nausea was gone. She moved her legs under her and felt strength return to her muscles. Raj took her elbow and helped her up.

The ground swam for a moment and she closed her eyes. Raj held her close, steadying her. She took a deep breath through her nose. "I'm fine." She took a step.

Professor Bahir gave One Eye some last minute instructions and then turned to the team.

"Let's make haste to Seagrove. Lace—" He shot her a look. "You're going to fly my old bones there."

What was he talking about? There was no way . . . she hadn't even tried . . . how could she mesh auras with Bahir . . . her mind stuttered at the problem.

Seeing her concern, Professor Bahir's face softened. "You can *try*. Now, everyone into your new clothes. And start thinking like a Centurion."

Lace curled her nose in distaste. "So we should think like a mass murderer who's been brainwashed by the King?" she asked. "Should we be ready to torture children and animals in order to get our way, or just men and women?"

"We'll do nothing evil, it will be a façade. We won't take it further than that," Professor Bahir said. "You know that."

Lace turned away—a bit embarrassed over her snide tone.

"I'll be a naturalist," Arif said, starting to peel off his clothes.

"Me too!" Violet said and threw her dress off, as if she'd been waiting for an excuse. Their bare skin gleamed in the sunlight. He was almost completely covered in colorful tattoos—Violet's skin was pink and clear as a baby's. She cooled an ember from the fire with the water, then smeared black kohl around her eyes, then smudged it on Arif's face. War paint. They looked fierce.

"I love their clothes." Arif put the necklaces on and adjusted the loincloth. He did a side kick. "Not stuffy at all."

"Right?" Violet threaded her fingers through the air, stretching. Her hair and the necklaces covered up her breasts. Mostly. But with Violet, the way she moved her body was so free and fluid that even though she was mostly naked she looked completely at ease. She was the kind of woman who fit her own skin very well.

"They're the perfect fit for you," Lace said. "We won't be so lucky."

The other Centurions' uniforms were fire red suits, with white linen shirts and stiff black shoes. It was hard to figure out who should wear which uniform.

Raj was the tallest and should have on the changer's

clothes, but Delia was short and round, her body covered with a thick layer of softness and so she needed the widest uniform. Lace limped over to one of the pale casters and picked up the clothes.

"I've always liked the Centurions' uniforms." Delia pulled on the red tailored pants lying on the ground. "I helped design a few of the details," she said with obvious pride.

A stream of derisive chides came into Lace's mind and she was about to spew them out when she realized that Delia had really had no say in her life before now. It's not like she wanted to be with King James. So she bit back her criticism.

Lace's clothes were baggy on her. She carefully slipped on the tunic so that it wouldn't touch her burn wound. Then she tucked her shirt into the trousers and put the suspenders over her shoulders. The loose neckline plunged, displaying the edge of her lacy chemise. At least this time the indecency of the clothes wasn't her fault. Once she put the fitted jacket on and buttoned it, she felt foreign in her own skin. Like she wasn't Lace anymore.

"This is me not saying anything about the fact that I had to change before coming and now we have to—"

Professor Bahir cleared his throat. "Thank you for rising above and not saying anything, Lace."

"You're welcome," she said.

She looked around at their troupe, and got a sinking feeling in her stomach. They weren't rebels anymore—they were Centurions.

Raj's shirt was a bit too small for him but she appreciated how it displayed the lines of his chest muscles. For a moment she just enjoyed watching him slip on the jacket and button it up, his face relaxed and pensive. His black hair was twisted tightly and his green eyes stood out against the red jacket. His arms were so long his wrists peeped out. Though she preferred him in his monk's garb, because that was just who he is, she thought him delightfully handsome in a uniform. What was it about men in a uniform that made her stomach go all wibbly-wobbly? When Delia caught her staring at Raj, she looked away.

"I think I have a problem," Cannon said, raising his arms in distress.

Lace's eyes caught Cannon and she laughed. "Your pants would fit Kaina better, I believe. Wait, they might even be too tight for Kaina." They were so short his white hairy ankles showed and the fabric stretched tightly across his thighs.

"Nice," Delia said sarcastically, but her eyes twinkled.

His eyes shone with mirth, then he jerked his hips one way then the other. "Oh, Lacey my dear, you've got to try on these snug pants they're just so comfortable. I think they're meant for you."

"No, no, no." She shook her head. "Nuh-uh, my ass wouldn't fit in them . . . and besides, can't you feel the power of tight pants?"

Cannon smoothed his hand along his leg and nodded. "I think I do. Like nothing can get past them."

"They're so tight a sword would just slide off," Lace said.

"So smooth that an arrow would bounce away." Delia smirked.

"Just watch out for your ankles," Raj said.

"Hear that?!" Lace announced loudly. "Everybody protect Cannon's ankles. Aye? *His ankles are sorely vulnerable.*"

"Aye!" everyone said, and even One Eye smiled.

Cannon laughed. Then his pants flared with magic— they elongated and widened, fitting just above his shoes. "Oy!" he said. "Magic pants."

Delia's hands glowed. "I can transform everyone's uniforms so they fit, if you want."

Oh, wouldn't that gift had been useful about five minutes ago? Why didn't Delia help them before they struggled into their uniforms? Lace sighed. She'd never understand that woman.

Delia sent magic to each outfit, elongating and slimming and widening each person's clothes so they fit perfectly.

"Aw," Cannon said. "I lost my power pants." Then he kissed Delia on the head.

Lace smoothed her hand along the jacket. She'd never worn such a nicely tailored jacket before. It felt perfect.

Delia surveyed her with pride. "I've never made an outfit for a brownie before, they are the ones that usually make them for me—" She stopped, cut off by the shocked expression on everyone's face.

"What?" Delia said.

Lace shivered with anger. "Don't you ever call me brownie. Ever again. Or call anyone else that! How could you?"

"What? Why?" Delia said, actually confused. Cannon shifted beside her, uncomfortable. For a long moment, Lace studied the woman. Delia's aura was clear—she really was not being malicious and that was the only thing that stayed Lace from running away from this company.

"You really don't know?" Violet said. "Gods! I thought you'd been *educated*. I haven't even been to school and I know that."

"She's been educated by people just like her," Raj said.

Professor Bahir eyed Lace. But she had this. Delia was being ignorant, not evil. Though ignorant still hurt, it was easier to deal with than evil. She took a deep breath.

"Delia," Lace said slowly, as if speaking to a toddler.

"Brownie is offensive—it's only used by oppressors, by those who don't want to see us as people. The name conjures up centuries of kidnapping, torture, slavery—no one else—"

"But I've heard brown people call each other that!" Delia exclaimed.

Gods, this woman did not know when to keep quiet.

"Really, I have," Delia looked from person to person, as if trying to get some acceptance. What she got were stony looks.

Lace snorted. "That's our right. But not yours. Believe me, no one with brown skin wants that name. Do you *promise* never to say such an awful word again?"

Delia nodded fervently. Her aura nearly broke with embarrassment and deep sadness. So when she said the words, Lace knew she really meant it: "I'm sorry, Lace. I won't ever say it again. I didn't know."

"I know you didn't." Lace broke the gaze with her—and gave a little laugh, trying to break the tension. "Or else I would be halfway to Zoto by now."

That brought another awkward silence, for it told the depth of the hurt. She looked down.

"Delia," Professor Bahir said, finally breaking in. "You'll need to wear a mask. Your face is too well known."

She nodded, as if eager for something to do. She tied two handkerchiefs together and then transformed them into a mask that covered her nose and mouth. Then she took one of the hats off the unconscious bodies and put it on her head. It was too big for her so she transformed it to fit. The rim shaded her eyes.

She looked mysterious. And dangerous.

"Won't I need to wear a disguise?" Arif put his hand on his sword. "I'm famous, too."

Everyone just blinked at him.

"I don't think you'll need one." Bahir held back a smile.

"But Black Sky is the terror of the sea. Merchants weep to hear his name. A legendary nightmare—" He looked earnest. "Don't you think someone will recognize me?"

Lace hid her smile behind her hand. "Aye, Black Sky has certainly haunted my dreams of late . . ."

"Even if someone recognizes you from the wanted posters," Bahir said. "They'll be too terrified to ask about it. We're Centurions. Now let's go."

Violet kissed One Eye on the cheek, then walked out of the ruins and down the trail.

Arif straightened up and shielded his eyes, gazing at the horizon. "I can't wait to be near her again."

"Focus, Arif," Professor Bahir said.

"Near who?" Delia asked.

"Near my only love. The sea." Arif started jogging down the tiny stone trail that led from the ruins to the main road,

Cannon at his heels.

Delia marched towards Lace with a bold expression and she mentally begged her to just keep her mouth shut.

No such luck.

Delia spoke in her know-it-all voice. Or maybe it was just her normal voice? "If you want to know how to carry Professor, don't carry his aura. You carry the air around him." Then she turned and made her way down the trail.

How did Delia think she could tell Lace what to do with *her* magic? The arrogance! That was—that was—wow. She was right. Carry the air's aura around him. Ah, so that was how it could be done. The whole theory suddenly fell in place. No need to blend his aura with hers at all.

She instantly formulated how she could control the air, trilling it with her fingers until the air around Bahir's back moved. It was easy to grip and manipulate.

It was not carrying him, it was more like carrying a basket of air that held him.

"How did Delia know that?" Lace asked, puzzled.

"You should ask her," Professor Bahir said. She had a feeling that he knew already. But a transformer's magic and an aura-controller's magic weren't the same at all. It was odd.

Her neck still throbbed and the pain was hot and intense, but she could work through it. She grabbed the air's aura around Professor Bahir and lifted. Her breath caught from the strain.

He rose, jerking his arms, unsteady. He gave her a weak grin.

"Ah-ha!" she exclaimed. "I *can* do it!"

Raj exchanged a warm smile with her.

It felt like dangling a fish in a net—except the fish was Bahir and the net was air. There was strain on her magic, but it wasn't too much.

"Will your magic hold all the way to Seagrove?" Bahir asked.

She nodded. "With a lot to spare."

Then she flew with him at her side down the incline towards the town. Raj broke into a run beneath them.

The ancient vineyards surrounding the town were beautiful. Tilled black earth under thick, neat rows with white fences separating the different varieties of grapes. She'd heard that Seagrove's wine was some of the finest in Dram.

They caught up with the students, and Lace slowed down. Bahir spoke. "Be sharp. Each of your gifts will be needed to solve the murder."

Cannon's face was troubled. "Not mine. Can't raise a dead person to life."

"Yours will be very useful," Bahir said in a chiding tone. "You're an expert of the body—you'll be able to tell us how she died."

"Let's go give her justice," Raj said.

Chapter Ten

Rotting from Inside

Seagrove had a tall, white stone wall around it, with watchtowers on all four corners. A few houses and shops lay outside the walls, but they looked closed up. The town lay low, at the bottom of the valley next to the scruffy docks. It was a small but prosperous region of Dram.

Gulls choked the beach, soaring and swooping in their frenzied, gawkish movements.

Boats were all moored on the docks, sails tightly wrapped, and not a fisherman was in sight. A few stray dogs lapped up fish scraps.

One lone, black flag was raised on the highest watchtower.

The students walked down the incline to the city.

"This place is in mourning," Violet said, closing her eyes

for a moment.

"This place is scared," Lace said. It reminded her of home—a town about to be invaded. They were scared of the most deadly people in Dram—Centurions.

The front gates opened with a low groan, and a shadowed figure in leather armor stepped out. He held a javelin and there was a short sword at his side.

"Lace?" Professor Bahir asked.

She studied the aura. "Not magical. He's scared," Lace said. "But he's not evil. He's a defender, won't attack unless provoked." Of that she was sure. What she wasn't so sure about was the next man coming through the gates. He had a thick head of black hair, which was pulled into a bun at the back of his neck. His resplendent royal blue robe reflected sunlight, and his aura was more . . . complicated.

She swallowed. "This man is a sly one, his aura's as wriggly as a worm. Some light and darkness in pieces of him, he's shallow, thus will be swayed by whatever is most helpful to him at the moment. He has a small magical item in his pocket—perhaps a timekeeper or something."

They were almost to the gate. The wall loomed above them and the cold shadow seeped into her skin.

"Hm," Arif said thoughtfully. "I'd never thought how auras would be helpful in battle, but now I see it. You can instantly understand your enemy."

Lace smiled. "You're more used to seeing your enemy's heart by cutting through their ribcage, aren't you?"

He chuckled and nodded.

"Set me down," Bahir said.

Straining the air's aura around him, she clenched her biceps and slowly lowered him. Once his knees bent she released the aura, and he steadied himself. She landed and walked in step beside him.

They approached the man, who opened his hands in greeting. His eyes were a steely gray. Light freckles dusted his nose. When they stood before him, his aura flared a scared orange. For only a moment. His eyes were caught on her and Raj—had he known there were no black apprentices coming? What if he knew the descriptions of the incoming apprentices?

But if he did, he made no indication of it.

Then he collected himself. "Welcome, apprentices. I wish you were here under better circumstances." He bowed low. "I am relieved to announce that we have caught the murderer. There's no need for you to investigate further. I humbly and deeply appreciate your presence, but we will execute the murderer and justice will be served."

Lace waited on Professor Bahir to set the mood. She looked at him from the corner of her eye, then did a double-take. His face was frozen except for bright rage glowering behind his dark eyes. His aura had hardened.

"Is that true?" Bahir said sharply. She nodded her head slightly. There was no lie in the man's aura. If he said he caught the murderer it was because he believed they caught the murderer.

"Who are you?" Bahir shouted.

The man stayed bowed low. "I am Maeve Copper. I am here to assist you."

"King James is horrified over the death of his Hierarch. You think you can perform this alone, you backwater sea crab? We will do the investigation on our own," Bahir said in such a low voice it was almost a growl. "Now take me to the murdered Hierarch."

The man bowed even lower, if that were possible. Then he backed up and turned and led them into the city.

Lace followed, full of trepidation.

***

The houses were tattered and worn, shutters firmly shut. No one was in the streets, and vendors' carts and craftsmen's stores were empty. If smoke wasn't pouring out of all the chimneys she'd have thought the town was deserted.

"Everyone's hiding," Delia whispered.

"From us," Lace said softly.

Because of the constant sand in the wind, whipping the houses, the paint was gritty and thin. The roofs had patched tiles and there were quite a few houses that were completely charred from the inside—burnt to ash.

There were remnants of wealth—ivory statues lining the street that were chipped and dirty, and a magnificent copper fountain, broken and covered in green slime. The place smelled like horse scad and moldy bread.

Lace scanned ahead, and her breath caught.

At the end of the road was a pink marble mansion with black iron gates barring access to it from the road. Before it stood a large, empty square, with stray cats placidly grooming themselves in its shadows. In the very center stood a towering split wood gallows.

Two bodies swung in the breeze.

One of the bodies was a young man, barely looked a day older than Lace. Above his head was a painted sign that read, TRAITOR.

It looked like more than one person in town had wanted to take down the Hierarch.

"This town is rotting from the inside," Raj said.

Chapter Eleven
Justice Will Be Done

Lace could see it in Raj's aura—he was horrified—he wasn't going to let this go. She pulled on his sleeve. "No, we didn't come to investigate that."

"But all lives are connected." He pointed to the decaying corpses. "If you think that those 'legal' murders don't have anything to do with the illegal murder in there—" He pointed at the castle. "Then . . ."

Lace understood. If there was trouble in the town—if people were being executed and leaving angry families behind—then it would affect the Hierarch greatly.

The bodies moved with slithering maggots and there were so many flies that a constant hum emanated, along with the stench. One of the men had white hair, long and traditional, while the other was young and had more of a modern, short haircut. They had to be related—both had wide, strong jaws and small eyes. Now sunken in and decrepit.

Bodies without souls were jarring to look at. It felt like a wounding blow to watch the corpses swaying, limp and gray, knowing that what made them human was gone.

"Excuse me, Maeve," Raj said.

Maeve stopped and folded his hands together. "Yes, Master?"

"Tell us about these executions," he said without even glancing at Professor Bahir. He had some guts to conduct an interview question without express permission.

Maeve bowed, as if that was what he did anytime he wasn't quite sure what to do. She saw in his aura that he was very uncomfortable with the topic, though his face betrayed nothing. "The man on the left was a notable wine barrel maker in town—but he didn't pay his taxes to the honorable King James and thus was executed for his treason." Maeve hesitated, then went on in a softer voice. "He was also accused of harboring mages."

It was illegal for any mages to be outside of King James' possession. The only mages in the country were slaves of the king, or worked for him. Once mages were discovered they were taken to the castle, and most were never seen again. It was a dangerous time to be born with magic.

"And the other man?" Raj asked.

"He was spreading lies about the Hierarch," Maeve said simply.

"What lies?" Professor Bahir said.

The presence of death was almost unbearable. She wished they could have had this conversation just inside the gate, rather than right at the feet of the gallows.

"He said that the Hierarch was supporting the village with her own money, paying King James herself rather than putting the burden on the villagers." Maeve gave a long sigh.

"Burden?" Cannon asked sharply. "You mean honor. It is an honor to support His Liege and back his noble enterprises." Lace almost smiled. That was a nice touch from Cannon.

Maeve startled. "Oh, of course. It's an honor, Master. A great honor."

"But that's impossible," Delia said. She hadn't looked at the bodies the entire time; she stared stolidly at Maeve. "King James mandates that each citizen must pay their dues themselves."

"They do," Maeve said, bowing again. "Every tax comes from the citizens' pocket or else they get a short rope and quick drop." But his aura tore at the lie.

Raj's aura darkened. "So the Hierarch executed this man for claiming she was taking care of the people from her own pocket?"

"Of course," Maeve said. He took a few steps backwards. "Shall we continue?"

Professor Bahir nodded and gestured that they should move on. The group slowly followed him, except for Raj, who was lost in thought.

Lace came up behind him, so close that she felt his warmth and smelled the heat of his skin. "What is it?" she asked.

He shook his head, as if to clear it, and then started walking. She followed him doggedly, continuing to stare at him, until he huffed through his nose. "Yes?"

"What is it?" she repeated.

"I want to know who murdered these men, and why."

"Then you should figure out who murdered those men, and why," Lace said.

He scratched his jaw and looked back at the gallows.

The palace gates were opened by two enormous, well-muscled guards. Their simple uniforms were tailored and covered expensive leather armor. Lace checked out their weapons, a bow slung over their back with a quiver at their hip, two sabers each, and throwing knives lining the belts. It'd take a lot to get past them. If somebody snuck in to murder the Hierarch, they probably didn't do it through the front gate.

Chapter Twelve
Opulence

They walked through impeccable gardens blossoming with honeysuckle, orchids, and shrubberies, which were trimmed into imaginative shapes by an overzealous gardener with too much time on his hands.

"Anything to do here besides trim bushes?" Lace whispered to Raj.

"I guess not."

Slaves waited on the stairs, lined up in a row and bowing as they approached. They wore starched gray uniforms. One of them, a teen girl, never stopped watching Lace as she climbed the steps. Her aura was strong and deep blue, a powerful friend and communicator, but it was rife with dark sorrow. She'd been affected by death. But which death?

In her hands was a pestle.

When Maeve neared her she approached him with her eyes down. She held out the pestle to him, which he took, and then he leaned in as she whispered something in his ear.

"Tell me what that is," Professor Bahir ordered.

Maeve turned around quickly. The girl slipped back into line, her shoulders shrinking, as if she wanted to become invisible.

"The girl found this in the kitchen this morning. It was empty but she thinks there was rockweed in it."

Lace had never heard of rockweed.

"Give it to our naturalist," Professor Bahir motioned with his hand to Violet. With caution, as if she would bite, Maeve brought the pestle to her.

She did look rather wild—with her frizzy hair bouncing around her head almost as if it had a will of its own. And her pink bare skin and her sharp, innocent eyes and the way the rune necklaces clacked together anytime she moved. Lace thought her wild beauty enchanting. Maeve treated her nakedness as if at the very sight of her he'd fall into hell.

First, Violet sniffed the white powder at the bottom of the pestle. Then she poked her finger in the dust and rolled it around her thumb, then a sliver of her tongue appeared and she tasted it. Making a face, she spit it out.

"For sure." She handed the pestle back to Maeve, who handed it back to the young girl. "It's rockweed. Dried.

Potent. Must have cost a fortune."

"What's rockweed?" Lace asked.

"Poison." Violet wiped her finger on her hip scarf thoroughly. "A teaspoon of it will have you unconscious."

"Whoa." Lace winced.

"It's a favorite poison in Dram mythologies," Cannon said. "It seems like most of the gods and goddesses have been poisoned by it in one story or another."

Delia spoke. Her voice was muffled by the mask. "Many hierarchs are fans of using it to assassinate their competition. I think they like to pretend they're one of the gods and goddesses."

"So that's how the hierarch was murdered?" Arif asked. "Poison?"

Maeve opened his mouth to answer, but Professor Bahir held up a finger. "Quiet. The evidence will tell us what we need to know. Now, lead us there."

Before they left down the hall, Lace memorized the young girl's face and aura, then slowed down so she could be in step with Raj.

They ascended the staircase and walked through an immense hallway with a huge canvas painting of a horse and lion on one end, and a collection of solid gold plates on the other.

"Perhaps if this Hierarch had sold a few of her gold

plates some of the villagers would have had food to put on theirs," Raj said under his breath. Lace nodded.

Their shoes tapped on the glistening floor. How was there no dirt or scuff marks? Someone had to spend all day or night cleaning them. Either that or everyone in the house had learned how to hover.

A vase of orchids on a small table lit the middle of the room with color.

This kind of opulence made her sick. How could someone live in such luxury while right outside the door people were in broken homes and no food? Though Hierarch Willow was a rebel spy, she did not have all her priorities right. Lace could *never* live like this.

Maeve paused before a room. His face paled a bit so that his freckles stood out even clearer. "This is where the murder took place."

"Let's see," Professor Bahir said.

They entered single file into a bathing room. The floor was warm. Underground coals, most likely. Half of the room was made up of a silver tiled pool, with a trickling fountain to one side. Blooming vines and flowers lined the wall beside the windows, which looked out to the glorious vision of the seaside.

Everyone gathered in the corner of the room. Lace's stomach churned at the sight.

Lying on a woven wicker chair was a woman in a robe. The flap was slightly open, showing one of her breasts. She had pure white hair, beautiful features, and bright red lipstick. Her eyes were open, frightened, and her mouth hung slack. Her forearms were prone, delicate wrists facing up. Bruises mottled her neck and arms.

A bloody dagger lay at her feet.

Chapter Thirteen
Clues

The knife handle was ivory, with a carved snake on one side.

Arif frowned and stepped close to the dead body. "I'm no physician but I believe the cause of death is a knife through the heart."

"So she was stabbed *and* poisoned?" Delia said. "Why both?"

Cannon stepped to the other side, his hands clasped behind his back, and peered closely at the woman's neck. Lace finally tore her eyes away from the body and looked around. A white towel lay on the other side of her chair and a leather knife sheath was lying beside the doorway.

Violet walked straight to the body and circled it. Her steps didn't make a sound. She stared at something above the corpse, not on it. *"A body is nothin', without the stuffin',"* she whispered. *"If the stuffin' ain't near, you're dead, my dear."* Was that a nursery rhyme? Lace had never heard of it. It was a bit harsh to quote at this moment.

"Maeve," Professor Bahir said. "How many residents are in this home?"

Maeve cleared his throat, then squinted and looked to the ceiling, as if counting. "Uh . . . eight servants and four family members."

"And you say you have found the murderer?" Professor Bahir said.

Maeve nodded. "Caught in the act. Our guards are getting more information from the murderer as we speak."

Bahir snapped his fingers and Maeve jumped. "Order the slaves into the hall and await my instructions."

Maeve bowed again and exited the room. His aura was dark with worry.

Once the man left Lace saw a remarkable transition in Professor Bahir. His aura started thinning and grew shallow, crumpling and filling with holes. Like it was decaying before her eyes. She longed to ask him what was happening, but knew she should wait until he chose to share. Nothing in Bahir's face revealed the turmoil, but the anguish was hard for Lace to watch.

She'd only seen this happen to this extent once before:

when her da was told that mother had been murdered in the caves.

"What is it, Lace?" Delia asked.

She blinked slowly, not realizing how transfixed she was by Bahir's aura, then looked at Delia. Was that—there was true concern in her question.

"You look troubled," Delia said.

Lace cleared her face, trying to waylay the question. Bahir's mental state was not her information to share. "It's just—" She swallowed. "It's hard to see a dead body."

"She doesn't appear to be tortured for information," Raj said.

"That's a relief," Delia said. "At least the rebellion is secret. So far."

Violet looked around, wide-eyed, taking in everything.

How would they ever be able to tell who the murderer was? They lacked context for every clue they found and knew nobody here—not only that but they had only a few hours before they'd have to leave.

The cards were stacked against them.

Raj said what she was thinking, "How long do we have?"

"We have until the sun is at its zenith to be back at the ruins and teleport out of here," Bahir said. That was about five hours. "Now," he said. "Collect details. There is nothing too small to mention. We must pore over everything in here and deduce what happened."

Arif slipped his shoes off and waded into the water.

"It's not really a good time to enjoy a nice soak," Lace said dryly.

"I'll check for anything in the water," he said, then dove under.

The bathing room was so humid it made Lace's burn feel worse. She wished she had a cool rag to press against the wound. Glancing at Cannon, she saw some of his magic had trickled back, but not much.

"She was posed." Raj motioned to the upturned hands. "Perhaps by the murderer. Or maybe the first person that came in and saw her."

Delia knelt before the woman and peered at her fingers, scrutinizing all the way up the arm. "She doesn't appear to have fought her attacker. No skin under the fingernails or bruises on the arms where she defended herself."

"So what does that mean?" Bahir asked.

"That she was either surprised by the kill, or . . ." Trouble darkened Delia's face. "That she knew the murderer."

"Did she know how to fight?" Lace asked.

Bahir nodded.

"I remember her dueling with another Hierarch in the gardens," Delia said. "She was also good with a bow. We practiced together a few times."

Arif popped out of the pool, clenching something in his hand. "This is out of place." He shook his long hair out like a dog, splattering water. Wading to the edge, he handed Bahir something small. "I'll keep looking." He dove back under.

Bahir held the item from Arif on the flat palm of his hand. It was a button made of bone. Delicate designs were carved into its face. One of a kind.

"Perhaps she struggled with the murderer," Delia said. "And the button popped off."

Cannon straightened and turned to the group. "She wasn't killed by the knife."

Chapter Fourteen
The Murderer

She wasn't killed by the knife? That's impossible.

Violet scoffed, "Can't imagine how she could survive it."

Cannon shook his head. "The knife was plunged in her heart after she was already dead."

That made no sense. Why would anyone do that?

"Are you sure?" Bahir asked Cannon.

He nodded. "If she was stabbed with the knife before she was dead, then her heart would still be pumping. Blood would be everywhere." Instead, there was just a little ring of blood around the wound. "But look here—" he pointed at her neck. "This neck bone is snapped in two and there's slight bruising under her jaw. She was strangled to death."

"But the angle's odd." Raj leaned down, peering up at the bruise, then moved his hands into a strangling position to show that there were no indentations. "And there's no finger bruises."

Lace pointed at the towel beside the chair. "That could be the murder weapon."

Raj nodded. Then frowned and shook his head. "The angle is wrong. It's as if the murderer were shorter than she was, choking high on her neck like that. If he or she were on top of her or taller than her, the marks would not look like that."

"So she was killed by a child?" Violet said.

Lace studied the door and the tiled wall, imagining what might have happened—different scenarios that would cause the strangling. The knife added a strange element to the mix. If she only knew how the scene played out, they might find more clues.

Lace walked to the wall and pored over the tiles, one by one. She pointed to a white hair caught on the damp surface. It was way above Lace's eye-level. "How odd."

Two hairs, obviously Willow's, were stuck on the wall. Delia came up behind Lace and scrutinized it. "She was strangled right here," Delia concluded.

"How do you know that?" Lace asked.

Delia took out her handkerchief and used it as a prop for the towel. She held her handkerchief tight between her hands and lifted it up as if strangling someone. "The murderer lifted her off her feet—thus the angle is so high on her neck."

Raj nodded thoughtfully. "Aye. That makes sense."

"Good thinking," Lace said.

"Good catch," Delia said.

And a bit of warmth passed between them.

"But the woman is no delicate flower," Cannon said. "Which means her attacker is tall and strong. Probably a man."

"So she was strangled, stabbed, *and* poisoned," Raj said. "Someone desperately wanted her dead."

A thought popped into Lace's mind. "It might not be her that was poisoned."

Arif burst out of the water. He took a deep breath. "Nothing more." Then he braced himself on the side of the pool and stepped out. Water streamed down his lithe body and slicked his hair back neat and straight.

Lace's stomach sunk at the thought of what had went on here. A lone woman, vulnerable, about to bathe—attacked by a man, possibly familiar to her. Strangled by her own towel.

Professor Bahir's aura was torn—she wondered if he had the strength to run this mission. Then she shoved that thought down. It was disrespectful. She promised herself she'd help him as well as she could.

The door burst open. It swung so fast the knob slammed

into the wall. A man charged in, face red, brows furrowed in rage, and tears in his eyes. He looked straight at Professor Bahir, finger pointed at him. "You!" he shouted. "YOU KILLED MY WIFE!"

Chapter Fifteen
Hierarch Spy

The man kept charging. Lace jumped in front of the professor, fists raised. Raj took the man's arm and swung him off balance, jarring him out of his attack. He jerked his arm but Raj's grip didn't loosen. "You aren't getting close to him," Raj said in a still voice. "Whatever you want to say, say it from here."

Panting in rage, he suddenly stepped back and noticed all the students in the room. And what they wore. He wilted a little and his posture subdued—that was when the tears spilled from the man's eyes. The first thing Lace noticed about his aura was that he was covered in anger, but there was deep grief behind it. And then she saw he had a bedrock gray of good spirit—he was no enemy. He had to be a family member of the dead woman.

Once he stopped struggling, Raj slowly let him go.

He had a bald, shiny head, pink skin, small stature, expensive clothes, and a thick beard, which was intricately braided. His age and stature reminded her a lot of Bahir.

"Get out of my house," the man said. "Now! You are never welcome here."

"Watch who you're talking to," Delia said. "We are sent from the king."

The man barked out a laugh. "Bahir no longer works with the King. And because of that, Willow is dead."

Bahir bowed slightly to the man. "Hierarch Stim. I have come with my students in order to find who killed Willow. It is of the utmost importance. Then I will leave you to your mourning in peace."

"Scad!" He wiped his wet cheeks. "You're here to protect your precious rebellion. You never cared about my wife." His voice rose in pitch, in emotion. "Why do you think she left you?"

Bahir's face showed a flash of turmoil. And then it went still.

"Now is not the time for this. What do you know, Hierarch Stim?" Bahir said. "Give us any information you have on what took place today."

Stim clenched his fists. "Good gods. We already caught the murderer, aye? Probably sent by King James because she

was spying for you. Haven't you done enough? Just go away."
He took a threatening step towards Bahir.

The professor strode forward, glowering. "You know
there will be major consequences. Especially now that the
war is about to start—you have no political sway."

"I'm not telling you anything," Stim yelled. "I'm taking
my family and we're leaving before the real Centurions get
here."

They stopped within a foot of each other, the tension so
sharp it crackled in the air. Lace tensed and fingered the knife
at her belt.

"No. You. Won't." Bahir's aura flashed with magic, but
then he calmed it. He stared at the man as if realizing what
he was doing. "Trust me. You'll stay here and answer any
questions we have for you. Get your family and stay in the
library. Wait for instructions."

Stim's aura damn near exploded in fury. "Mages!
Always forcing themselves on non-magical people. You
aren't going to tell me what to do in my own home!" his voice
cracked. "My wife is dead. The Centurions are coming. At
least let us flee in peace."

Bahir's voice softened. He took a step back and the
intensity on his face retreated. "I have experience in these
matters. If you want to survive the hell King James is about
to unleash, do as I say. Arif, why don't you guide Stim and

the rest of his family to the library?"

Arif stepped forward with his hand resting on the handle of his saber. His lithe body was still wet from the pool.

"I'm not taking that naked man near my granddaughter!" Stim said.

"You'll do what you're told," Arif snapped. His hands flared with golden magic, and Stim took a step back. "We're here to calm the storm coming your way, and protect dozens of lives. If you care anything for your wife and the rebellion she stood for, you'll do everything we tell you." Arif created a ball of swirling mist and threw it at Stim.

The cloud surrounded Stim with gray tendrils. It was harmless, only a show of force.

Stim's face flushed and he opened his mouth to say something. His eye suddenly caught Willow in the chair. A wave of remorse went over him and he trembled, holding back strong emotions. He couldn't look away from the cold, still body. It broke him.

He turned and walked out of the room. Arif followed at his heel.

A deep silence settled over them after he left.

Lace had a thousand questions tumbling in her mind— why had Bahir and Willow parted ways? And what is Willow's role in the rebellion? And had she endangered any of them before she died?

"Professor," Cannon said. "Do you think she told anyone about the rebellion?"

They waited in the warm room, with only the trickle of water from the fountain. As if a nervous habit, Violet opened her hand and closed it, furling and unfurling a flower connected to the wall.

"We will soon find out," Bahir said sharply. "Lace, Raj— go find out who the suspected murderer is. Gather all the information you can, and talk as little as possible. Understand?"

They nodded at the same time.

"Remember, you're a Centurion assistant," Delia said with an edge to her voice. "Don't be sweet, Lace."

Lace nodded and pulled her wrist sleeve down and looked at Raj. He opened the door and motioned her through. As she walked past him their auras mingled, as if drawn by a magnet.

She had a hundred more questions than when she went into the room. How could they ever solve the murder in time?

Chapter Sixteen

The Murderer and the Lie

Maeve and the slaves were still waiting in the hallway. Their feet were probably getting sore by now. The slaves stood at attention, staring ahead as if they blocked everything out. It was creepy how the masters not only treated them as property, but actually wanted to make them act as a piece of furniture would.

She strode down the row until she reached the young lady whose aura was so bright and emotional Lace guessed that she knew the deceased well or was involved somehow. "You." She met the girl's eye, which stared down at the floor. "Where are they keeping the murderer?"

The girl didn't move or speak.

Maeve had probably threatened them and told them if they did, they'd face some kind of punishment. It was as if

Raj read her mind, because he told Maeve in his soft, harsh voice, "Tell her to do whatever the Centurion wants."

"Answer her," Maeve's voice rang out.

The girl quickly nodded. She was very tall, with cropped curly hair, smooth brown skin, and bone-white earrings. Looking down the row of slaves Lace saw that all of them wore earrings, men and women. A mark of their servitude.

"Take me there," Lace said and stepped back. The girl strode forward and walked down the hall.

"Please, sir, let me—" Maeve sputtered.

"Come with us," Raj said to him.

Lace followed half a step behind the girl, who kept a fast pace. The house's floor was gleaming marble, she could see reflections in it—Lace didn't think she'd ever seen the palace floor in Zoto so clean. Probably because the royal children had to sweep and mop it themselves. And she barely had enough patience to sweep the front hall, much less all the halls.

There was dark wood trim carved in elaborate designs framing every wall and window and door. Decadent. Like colored frosting on a cake.

They turned a corner. Lace caught the girl looking out of the corner of her eye.

"What is your job here?" Lace asked.

She had a soft voice, laced with worry. "I used to be a

house maid, but since Master Jon came back I am his child's caretaker." Her Dram accent was flawless—perhaps she had been born in the country, not kidnapped as most slaves had been.

"Is Master Jon Hierarch Stim's son? The professor?"

She nodded.

"Why aren't you with the child now?"

A flash of worry creased her young face. "Last night her father told me that he wanted to care for her." She set her lips.

"Is that normal?"

Their footsteps were muted as they crossed a thick, colorful carpet.

"No," the girl said.

They came to another corner and Lace realized they were heading to the back of the house. They passed huge dining rooms, large windows, plush parlor furniture, and immense paintings until they came through a door into a smaller hallway, where the ceiling was lower and the floors were wood, not marble.

That was when she heard it.

The attack.

The sound of whip on skin—that whistle of speed, slap of leather, cry of soul. Lace broke into a run and burst through the wooden door. It opened so fast it slammed against the hinges.

In the middle of a small courtyard there was a woman tied to a post. A carriage house was on one side of the courtyard, and three horses were tied to a hitching post, with a large stable behind it. A porch wrapped around the brick courtyard.

Her eyes fixed on the figure tied to a post in the middle of the yard. The woman's body braced against the whip, every muscle strained and tightened. They'd taken her shirt off—her smooth back shone bright in the heat. Her aura was swollen pink with misery.

One man, wearing the Hierarch's uniform, was at the woman's face asking her questions, "Who are you working with?" he shouted. Another man was behind her, beating her with a slim leather whip.

Lace lunged off the porch and grabbed the air, flying as fast as she could, overcome with the pain on the woman's face. At the quick movement the burn on her neck exploded in pain. Just as the man brought the whip down Lace landed in front of it.

The leather cut through the air. She didn't have time to attack or protect herself. Lace raised her arms above her head, flinching.

But just as the whip came down on her back, it disappeared.

The guard gasped. Lace looked up and saw Raj with the whip in his hand. His aura glowed with magic.

Clever man. He'd reverse-summoned the whip.

"Aye, what?" The guard exclaimed and drew his sword. He had a confused look on his face. Lace took a menacing step towards him. His eyes widened in fear. Suddenly he didn't see her gender, her height, or her age—all he saw was King James' insignia on her red jacket and neck. The most dangerous symbol in the world. It was all that mattered.

The guard bowed low. When the other guard saw them he stumbled back, muttering in confusion. The young girl leapt from behind Raj, reaching for the woman tied to the post, but Raj held her back. Maeve stayed shadowed in the doorway.

Lace wrenched the sword out of the guard's hand and threw it across the courtyard. It hit the barn wall with a thud, its handle wavering from the force.

What had they done to this woman?

There were at least six welts on her back. Blood seeped from them. Her shoulders rose and fell in deep breaths, and her legs trembled. A dark, jagged root cut deep in her aura, as if she'd just been through a soul-searing experience that broke who she was. It was exactly the kind of aura she'd seen in murderers.

No one, not even a murderer, deserved to be tortured

like that.

Lace's heart beat wildly in her chest and her skin buzzed with a flow of adrenalin. Every thought fled, for right now she wasn't an ally or defender, she was supposed to be a ruthless warrior.

She certainly felt like hitting something.

Raj's face was a wall, smooth and tranquil. Just looking into his eyes calmed her. "How dare you start the interrogation without our consent!" she said.

"Your grace," the guard said, head still bowed. "My deepest apologies."

"How do you know this woman is the murderer?" Raj asked.

Though the woman had a splintered aura, it didn't make her guilty. Many things could cause that.

The guards stayed bowed. The bald one with a whip said, "She was caught by—"

"I can't hear you, stand up!" Lace ordered him.

He straightened, and Lace saw in his aura how confused and upset he was. "She did it. It *was* her! Caught by Mistress Mary and a maid when they went to bathe this morning. They found her with the knife in her hand, standing over the body."

"Red handed," the other guard added dumbly.

With the knife that hadn't really killed Willow.

"Did they actually see her plunge the knife in the Hierarch?" Raj asked.

The guard shook his head. Then shrugged.

"Did she confess?" Raj asked.

"She hasn't said anything." The guard wiped sweat off his forehead. "Not a damn thing. Master Stim said he was going to execute her himself at noon." When he saw Lace's contempt, he bowed again and quickly added, "According to your good pleasure, Mistress."

Raj and Lace exchanged a look. It wasn't unthinkable to believe that a slave would kill her mistress. After all, the masters and mistresses had taken *her* life. But Lace felt in her gut that this was too clean. Too easy. They had to know more.

"Untie her," Lace said sharply. "Then get out of here! I don't suffer fools."

The guard stepped forward and fumbled with the ropes binding the woman's hands. When they fell to the ground, the woman took her tunic with shaking hands, and slipped it over her head. There were no buttons on the shirt, none that matched the one Arif had found. Her shoulders were solid muscle and her arms firm and rounded—she *was* strong and tall enough to strangle Willow. Then Lace noticed the scars.

Beautiful, deep scar lines curled down the woman's

neck. And it wasn't a slave brand. It was a mark of the *Vingiz* tribe, a country west of Zoto. The land was famous for its metallurgy and fine music, mostly harps and stringed instruments. She'd visited on a dignitary's trip with Da, and had been amazed at the intricate scar tattoos on the women and men's bodies.

This woman had been kidnapped. It was a common practice for Dram traders. For a minute she was so angry all she could do was clench and unclench her fists, taking quiet breaths, just so she wouldn't go crazy.

She wanted to crush this place. Crush this system. Crush this country. Gods, she wanted to so bad. How could anything this evil survive? Breathe, she told herself. Calm down. It'll all be okay. Deal with that later. Her heart started a steady rhythm again.

The guards hastened out the door.

Raj looked at her and nodded. His aura flared blue with compassion though his face didn't reveal anything. He could read what she was going through.

Maeve stepped out of the shadows. "Sylvia, Sylvia," he said. She clasped her hands before her and lowered her eyes. "Make things clear to these Centurions. Did you or did you not murder your mistress?"

There was a pause and everyone held their breath as they waited for the answer.

"Yes," Sylvia said. "I did."

The young girl gasped and covered her mouth with her hand. "You wouldn't!" wrenched out of her.

Lace couldn't believe her. She couldn't because the moment Sylvia had confessed, her aura split.

The confession was a lie.

Chapter Seventeen
Listening

"Who are you?" Lace asked her, needing to see an answer to a simple question so she could see if her aura reading was off.

"I am Sylvia," the woman said. "I am—was," she corrected herself, "Hierarch Willow's personal maid."

She was surrounded by a pure, golden aura . . . complex and nourishing and good. With that dark agony root in the middle—was her mind unstable? How was she both at the same time? Whoever she was, it didn't matter if Lace knew she was lying unless she knew why.

Lace squinted, trying to feel what went on in the complex aura in front of her. Why admit to the crime if she didn't do it? There had to be more to it. And Lace had to find out what it was. Sylvia's life was at stake.

"Follow us," Lace said. "We're bringing you to meet *our* master."

***

There had to be a way Lace could figure out Sylvia's motive. If she was lying about killing Willow, then who was she trying to protect?

The wind blew through and ruffled Lace's hair—it smelled of hay and wood. With a hint of that sweet horse smell. Sharp shadows cut lines across the floor, creating patterns.

Time was moving fast. Too fast. They had to solve this soon!

The young girl started crying. Tears rolled down her cheeks and her bottom lip trembled. Little sobs escaped her.

Sylvia followed Lace, shoulders back, chin up.

The young girl ran to Sylvia when they approached. She gripped her and Sylvia put her arms around her shaking shoulders, whispering soothing words.

Raj leaned in to Lace, placing his hand on the small of her back. He whispered in a voice full of sarcasm, "We've caught the evil murderer. But it feels anything but right."

"Aye. Now the whole town may get off the hook as long as her and her family suffer horribly." Her hair grazed his cheek.

Something must have crossed her expression because he

asked, "What is it?"

She leaned in even further, so their shoulders touched. "She's lying."

Raj glanced quickly at Sylvia. "What?"

"She's lying," Lace whispered. "She didn't kill—" she stopped when she saw Sylvia and Maeve staring at her. Lace turned her face so the woman couldn't read her lips. "I don't know why, but she's confessed to something that she didn't do. It's not clear why."

"Are you sure?"

"No. But I'm pretty sure." Lace put her hands in her jacket pockets. "Unless her soul is really abnormal."

"Why would she willingly put herself in this position?" Raj asked. Their faces clouded at the thought of what was to come.

Sylvia held the young girl wrapped in her arms, sobs filled the air. Her brown eyes were on Lace and Raj— watching them as closely as a bird watches a snake.

Once the Centurions arrived they'd torture her for days. They'd slowly kill her family and friends in front of her. They'd parade her back to the capitol and then have a huge public execution. Anyone who harmed a hierarch was considered a traitor and traitors were made into a spectacle. Which is why it so rarely happened. Which was why they had to keep Willow's role in the rebellion a secret.

Raj paused, with a thoughtful expression. The light reflected off his eyes, causing the green to shine.

"We'd better return her to Professor," Lace said. "Maybe he'll be able to figure out why she'd lie . . . if she's lying."

Raj squinted, doubting.

"You have a better idea?"

"Professor didn't say return the suspected murderer, exactly." Raj leaned down again to whisper close to her ear. "He just told us to find out who the murderer was. What if . . . what if we . . . what if we got her to talk?"

"I'm not taking her back to the whipping post, if that's what you—"

"No!" His eyes took on a thoughtful, glassy gaze. "We need her to-to-to relax, to talk to someone she trusts, and we hear it. Add a wall . . . She has to tell someone—and then I can use my new trick and—"

Lace had to hold back a smile as Raj's brain was working faster than his mouth. "You're talking but you're not making sense."

He snapped his fingers. "I know! Got it!"

He ran to Maeve and demanded a question that Lace couldn't hear. The man gave him a key and he returned, his strong, sure steps eating up the distance. "Let's go." Without waiting to see if she was following, he hurried through the doorway and down the hallway.

What was he up to?

"Follow him," Lace told Sylvia. She looked over her shoulder at Maeve. "You. Meet us back in the main hallway."

He bowed deeply. But she saw his aura flare in annoyance.

The young girl wouldn't let go of Sylvia's arm. Lace walked behind them, hand on her hilt, ready in case they attacked Raj or tried to escape. She didn't think they seemed dangerous, but they were desperate and scared. Two ingredients in a recipe for violence.

The best way to get harmed was to believe, 'they'd never do that,' and take no precautions. So she kept her knife at ready.

Chapter Eighteen
The Trick

Raj brought them down a long brick hallway full of rooms with closed doors. This part of the house smelled old and dank, as if the windows were never opened. Judging by the identical rooms to the bare floors, she assumed they were the slave quarters.

The women tensed up the further along they went. Which made Lace tense up.

Raj leaned over a doorknob and unlocked it with the key. Then he opened it and ushered the women inside. Lace peeked in and saw two simple mattresses on the ground with threadbare quilts, a clay pitcher on the floor, and a bucket. There were no windows.

The young woman cowered. "This isn't our room," she said.

"Get in," Raj said sharply.

Their heads both snapped down and they shuffled forward. As soon as they crossed the threshold, Raj slammed the door shut and locked it. Then he tested the strength of the door. It stayed solid.

"What're you—?"

"Sh!" Raj held up a finger. He cocked his head. Everything was silent behind the door. "Let's go talk to Professor." Why was he speaking so loud? He turned and headed back down the hall, his footsteps made loud thumps on the wood as he walked away.

Lace rolled her eyes and followed. He was being cryptic. She lost sight of him at the end of the hallway when he turned, and then she almost crashed into him when she crossed the corner. "Whoa." She jolted to a stop.

He gripped her arms. "Now we go back." Though his mouth was as serious as ever, his eyes sparkled as if barely holding back a secret. "Quietly."

Taking her hand, he crept down the hallway. Her soft-soled sandals were silent on the smooth tiles. For a second she enjoyed the joy of the being led along.

They got back to the door and they faced it. Lace looked at him expectantly. He held up a glowing finger, closed his eyes, and then wrote something in the air. His hand glowed blue. There was a powerful spell in the air.

Nothing happened.

Raj opened his eyes slowly, disappointed. She raised her eyebrows and tried to hold back a smile. *Impressive,* she mouthed. He shook his head and tried again. His hands glowed blue and he sighed a word again. And again.

Still, nothing.

She crossed her arms across her chest. What was he trying to do?

Frustrated, he made a grand, sweeping motion with his hand. A whisper came out of the blue magic. Half of a sentence—*how could you*—then it silenced.

Lace's mouth fell open. That was Sylvia's voice.

Bright eyed, Raj made the motion again and this time he held the blue between his hands, not letting go. Voices came out of the empty space. *We have to get you out of here.*

"Is that—" she whispered. "Are you summoning voices?"

He nodded without taking his eyes off of the blue magic.

That was incredible. They could hear what Sylvia was saying to the young girl, when they thought they were alone. She leaned in, listening. The voices flickered in and out of hearing.

"How could you? How could you possibly . . . ? Mistress Willow was so important . . ."

"*. . . I got nothing else now.*"

"*Like hell! You think I'm nothing? How can you go through with this? You know what they do to traitors—*"

"*I know, dammit. I know . . . thought of . . . before I confessed and—*"

The voice was lost. Blue magic cleared into nothing. Raj's forehead was shiny with sweat. He made the rune again in the air and the voice came back.

"*. . . I was with her—*" Sylvia was saying.

"*Gods, why?*" the young girl nearly shouted.

"*Jon told me to.*"

"*Master Jon? I don't understand. Why would he tell you to stay with her last night . . .*"

They broke off again and Raj set his lips and made the sign again.

"*. . . you've got to fight this, it's not going to stop. Things will just get worse and worse for us until . . .*"

There was a pregnant pause.

"*Listen. That worm ridden bastard King James stole my children and destroyed my village. And Stim let it happen. If I can keep three—*" She cut out "*. . . more away from him, then I'll die in peace. And I'm going to go the rest of my life without calling anyone else master or mistress, so I'll die with my honor.*"

No! Sobbing broke through. *No! You can't leave me. You can't go through this alone! I love you. I love you so much.* The agony in her shaking voice brought tears to Lace's eyes. *Why can't you tell them what you saw?*

The last words came through strong and loud.

I'll go to King James' dungeons before I let that happen.

Chapter Nineteen
Space

The conversation faded off, leaving Lace more confused than ever.

It erupted more questions than answers. Who was Sylvia protecting? And if she loved Willow, then why would she protect the murderer?

They needed to find out more about who this woman was. But now was not the time to do it. Here, Sylvia was safe and they couldn't risk taking her out again to meet Professor Bahir.

Raj started to walk down the hallway but Lace snapped her finger. He turned. She pointed to the lock and whispered, "There might be a second key. I don't want anyone to break in and hurt Sylvia. Can you—?" Before she could finish her sentence his hands glowed blue and he'd transported some kind of cloth or padding into the lock so no key would fit.

She gave a sharp nod, then followed him down the hall. No one else was going to die. Not on her watch.

***

On their way back, Raj pulled her into a small corner room. It was a parlor or sitting room or some such purposeless space. "How inane," she muttered, looking around at the uncomfortable furniture and oversized decorations. "What is this room even *for*?"

But his gaze wasn't on the room—he shifted, and ran his hand through his dark, coarse hair.

She looked up into his eyes. "What is it?"

He studied her face, lips tense, as if about to say something important. Then he sighed and pointed to the corner. "A shortcut. Let's get back to the group so Cannon can heal your neck. It looks so painful."

Sure enough, a small, low-ceilinged hallway lay hidden in the shadows. It was barely noticeable, situated behind a tall wardrobe.

Her lips parted in wonder. "How did you know this was here?"

Taking her hand, he made for it. "I have a pretty good sense of space."

Her fingers curled around his. His brown skin was lighter than hers, by a few shades. "*And* you can summon sound . . ." she paused. "Which is useful, but invasive. Good thing you're a monk full of integrity and honesty and would never spy on me or anything. Or show up uninvited while I'm taking a bath, that would just be—"

"About that," he interrupted, looking at her from the corner of his eye. And then he gave an almost imperceptible wink.

The hallway was dim except where the light at the end shone through, their footsteps were soft on the rich wood floor.

"Well?" She laughed. "Tell me about it, what was that? Do you often do that to women in the middle of the night? When they aren't even wearing bed clothes?"

That word sparked something in her, as if she should remember it. But why? Raj's words drove the worry from her mind.

"That was a first," he said lightly. When she glanced closer at him she could tell his cheeks were warm. "I—I'm sorry, I was just told to imagine what . . ." He trailed off.

She helped him out. "We were told to imagine our powers out of the box."

He nodded, not quite looking her in the eye.

"And so you reverse summoned yourself?" she prompted, curious.

He nodded again. "It brought me to the source of my

thoughts."

"Me?" she blurted out, surprised.

He was breathing quicker now, and sped up his pace. "My thoughts are often on you."

She swallowed, pleased, and a warmth spread over her.

"How are you?" he asked suddenly, changing the subject. "It is hard being here, isn't it? Seeing the way they live. Do you need anything?"

For a second she just studied the slope of his jaw as he looked at her. Then she caught herself and swallowed. "You don't have any water on you, do you?"

A glass of water appeared in front of his nose. It fell and he caught it smoothly, then handed it to her. She stopped and drank the whole cup. With a deep breath, she handed the glass back and wiped her lips with the back of her hand. The water was cool and fresh. "Thank you."

The cup vanished in front of him. "So you know space?" she asked, still in awe of how he knew this passageway was here.

"Not always," he said. "When I was little, the caves were my world. I knew where everything was, down to even the flies and geckos and gold veins in the rocks. After you and your mother saved me from the mage, I was taken to the monks." He paused. "The world was vast and horrifying."

She listened carefully.

"Suddenly I couldn't measure everything." His voice was so sad. "Couldn't read the space above me. When they tried to take me outside, especially at night, I'd have panic attacks and run away. I'd want to bury myself in the rocks. Then . . . then my new father, he gave me a paper star chart and taught me the constellations one at a time, helping me memorize them. I became curious, and my longing to see the stars outweighed my fear. So one clear night when the stars were brilliant and glimmering in star-speech, I went out there. And since I had the map I knew . . ."

"You could measure them," she said.

He nodded.

"And now space is yours."

They came out of the tunnel, ducking through a tapestry, and walked into another sitting room. A slave boy was there, sweeping and humming quietly to himself. He startled when they came out of the shadows. Raj quickly let go of her hand.

And she felt the space between them acutely.

***

Cannon met them in the grand hallway. "There you are!" he exclaimed to Lace, reaching for her. "Let me heal you."

Lace gave a crooked grin. "I wouldn't ever say no to a good healing. Thank you."

They paused on the plush violet carpet, and Cannon glanced at Raj. "Professor Bahir wants you."

Raj nodded, and headed for the bathhouse, leaving them alone in the vast, high-ceilinged hall.

Cannon took her hand—his fingers were long and nails well-manicured, like all noble-born. They were infinitely gentle and tender, as if he knew the exact power every touch needed.

Delicious tingles spread up her arm, crackling like fire, but the feeling gave refreshment, not pain. The magic settled on her neck and she closed her eyes in relief, giving a small moan. Her flesh was knitting together, smoothing, renewing.

"All better?" Cannon asked, still holding her hand.

She breathed a heartfelt sigh and touched the scar on her neck. It felt as normal and well as anywhere else. "Thank you, Cannon." Squeezing his hand, she let go and started down the hall.

"Wait," he said. She looked back. He shifted, nervous, and tugged the uniform's sleeve. "Can we talk about Delia for a second?"

Uh-oh. What was he going to say? He and Delia had a bond stronger than almost any Lace had ever seen—if he felt she'd mishandled things—

He interrupted her thoughts. "Delia can be a bit of an ass."

A surprised laugh burst from her.

"But," he continued, "once she accepts you, you'll never find a better friend—though she'll always be the first to tell you when you're wrong, she'll always be the first to tear up anyone who tries to hurt you."

Lace looked at him quizzically. Why was he telling her this?

He ran his fingers through his blond hair and sighed. "What I mean is, please don't give up on her yet. She's been through hell and—"

Lace interrupted, "Everyone's been through hell."

Cannon held his hand up. "I know, my dear. I know. Not making excuses." His expression sharpened. "Just begging you not to give up on her."

She thought of Professor Bahir, and what he'd said to her last night. To be friends with Delia. No matter how much Delia disgruntled or frustrated Lace, she was in her life. And Lace had to decide . . ." There are a lot of things I respect about her," Lace said, then bit her lip. "Don't worry. We're stuck together. I'll not abandon her."

Cannon's face split into a grin that made his blue eyes shine. "You're precious," he said. "Thank you."

She slowly shook her head as they turned down the hallway. "You're a healer through and through, aren't you?"

He looked around, eyes sad. "I wish I could heal

everything."

***

Lace and Raj told the group everything about Sylvia. She watched as each of their faces reacted in concern at the beating and then confusion at the confession.

Lace turned to Professor Bahir face to face. "If we need to find out who murdered the Hierarch, we must find out why. Why would someone want to kill her?"

For a moment all that was heard was the trickling of the fountain as Bahir mulled everything over. The stillness in the home and in the town was unsettling—no buzzing of conversation or footfalls or the thrum of daily activity. Nothing. Only the soft whistle of the wind on the window.

Finally, Professor Bahir sighed and looked up. "It's all about money."

Lace clenched her fist. "Scad. Of course it is."

Raj frowned. "Every sinister root in our society is fed by greed."

"What's *that* life worth?" Violet pointed to the dead woman.

"Millions," Bahir said. "She's the core of this town. This leads to the dead men hanging on the gallows. Willow told me about the horribly unfortunate injustice."

"For the past ten years," Professor Bahir said, "Seagrove has been sinking under the weight of King James' taxes. The grape vines are actually faring better than ever, and the wine makers are still selling their bottles to every town in Dram . . . but the town has gotten poorer and poorer as the taxes are raised higher and higher. Then three years ago there was a dry season and they lost half their grapes and even fishing took a blow." He sighed. "But everything climaxed last year when the war tax was levied on them and more than half the town couldn't pay it!"

That war tax was for the effort to invade Zoto and all the eastern lands.

Delia gasped. "How did they survive?"

Professor Bahir lowered his voice. "Willow gave her entire life savings and family jewels to pay the war tax for everyone."

Lace swallowed. That was a brave move.

"Stim wanted no part in it, but she charged on. Sold all their horses but four. Sold every extra slave they had. Sold heirlooms and art, while still trying to save face before the King and act like everything was normal. But time was running out. She secretly arranged for her step-son, Jon, to be released from his duty as a professor, fearing King James would take it out on him once the secret was known."

"She couldn't keep that act up for long," Raj said.

Professor Bahir started to say something, but his throat caught. He cleared his throat and took a deep breath, then said, "She was waiting for us. For our rebellion to succeed."

He looked around at each of them. "Many people are. They are waiting for us to defeat the king."

The enormity of what she was getting into struck her. Being a part of the Magic Academy wasn't just a way for her to improve her craft, to save Zoto, or to get back at the King. It was a mission that would change the whole world.

Gods, that made her feel small and big at the same time.

"What does money have to do with the hanging men?" Cannon asked. "Did Willow steal their money?"

"Willow was under an enormous amount of stress—trying to juggle helping the people and keeping her job as Hierarch—then one day everything collapsed. The main wine barrel maker was at the gates with a frantic crowd, not able to pay his already-reduced taxes—and another Hierarch was visiting from the capitol. The Hierarch pressured her into acting, and she knew she couldn't ignore it. She knew she had to do something to save face with the capitol, so he was executed right then. His son attacked the guards, yelling at Willow that he thought she was on their side. So she executed him as well. But still, she thinks the visiting Hierarch suspects something and told King James about it."

"Scad," Raj whispered.

Silence engulfed them. It was all gray. On the one hand, how could anyone change the capitol for good without rising in power like Willow did, but on the other hand, she had to compromise so much to keep that power.

"You think that cost her life?" Lace asked.

Delia looked thoughtful. "What if Stim killed her for going against him? For putting his title in danger? Men have killed for less."

"How could he kill his own wife?" Violet asked. "He didn't seem the type."

"Anyone is capable of murder," Lace said in a low voice. She looked around at each of them. "Everyone in this room has killed someone—" Their faces grew solemn. "Whether justified or not, given the right circumstance, there is murder in *every* soul."

Chapter Twenty
Trust

Lace tried to fit this story into the bigger picture. "So if Willow executed those men, then he'd have an angry family left behind."

"And an angry village," Arif added.

"Murderous, even," Violet said. "*A town's trust takes years to gain, one second's mistake and it's all in vain.*"

Lace *did* know that rhyme. It was in one of the Drammian books Lace had read as a child when her tutor was teaching her to learn the language.

Raj paced to the door and back. "What do we do now?"

"Delia and Lace," Professor Bahir said softly. "Please go to Stim and his family. I'd like you to interview them about where they were during the murder, find out about anyone who might have wanted to kill her, or any strange occurrences they've noticed lately. And then I'll interview her lady's maid and—"

"Slave," Lace interrupted.

"What?" Bahir said.

"Lady's slave." Lace indicated outside the room. "Call them what they are."

Bahir nodded. "I'll interview Willow's slave. She will probably have more information about what happened this morning than anyone else. Which reminds me, while you're there please instruct Stim to write papers of emancipation for each of his slaves. Then they'll be able to flee anywhere and no one can stop them."

"But what if Stim recognizes me?" Delia said, touching her mask. "We met quite a few times while I was still Queen."

"I know," Bahir said. "Which is why you are there to observe Lace. She is the one who can see auras, so she knows who's lying or when they're pushed too far. You're only there to observe."

Delia objected, which seemed as natural to her as breath. "But what if I need to tell—"

"Observe," Bahir interrupted. "*Listen.* That's your only role. Don't speak at all. Do you understand?"

She gave a quick glance to Lace and her aura flared with nervousness. But there was no hint of anger or disgust, which surprised Lace.

"Listen, don't speak," Bahir said again.

"I understand." She straightened her shoulders.

"Cannon, Raj, Violet and I will collect more clues here, then interview Sylvia. In thirty minutes we'll meet in the butterfly garden and go over what we've learned. We only have three hours left, so hurry!"

***

When Lace stepped into the brilliant white hall her chest tightened. Out of everyone in the team, Bahir had chosen her to lead the interview. It lifted her up and terrified her at the same time. With that kind of responsibility, she'd be the first to blame if something went wrong.

The hallway was much hotter than the bathing room. Sunlight streamed through the windows and baked the marble floors—roasting everything on it like bread. And what little ventilation they had wasn't enough to let the cool wind inside. Lace was instantly coated in sweat—although that might also have been from nerves.

But she didn't have time to be nervous—there was Maeve, coming right up to her.

"How may I assist you?" he asked.

Slaves lined up behind him, against the wall. Sweat coated their faces and dripped off their chin. They looked stiff and uncomfortable. And their auras glowed with fear.

She knew next to nothing of this society, of this culture.

Of the rich. What did these slaves even do all day? Lace's family had never even had servants—they did all their own work. And Zoto's 'castle' could fit in the main entryway. This culture was Delia's domain.

If only she could rely on Delia for more than just intense glares.

But she needed an ally. Or at the very least, a guide.

She spoke in a loud voice so her words echoed through the hall. "Who is Stim's steward?"

One older man stepped forward, eyes down, and walked up to Lace. His aura was deep and blue, compassionate and intelligent. He was not afraid, but there was a streak of rage hiding under the surface of his soul. Like most slaves had. His curly hair was cropped, his brown skin was freckled around his nose, and his gait was confident and purposeful. Lace liked him already.

"What are you, stupid?" Lace said severely to Maeve. "Excuse these slaves. I don't want them watching our investigation." Maeve looked confused at her words. He held up his hand, his aura bright with concern. Lace raised her eyebrows.

He froze.

"Yes?" she asked in her most haughty tone.

"Might I assist you?" Maeve asked. "As it is my duty?"

There was no way she could trust Maeve. His interests

were too divided.

"No, you may not." She turned to the steward. "Take me to Hierarch Stim."

The man bowed deeply, then led the two ladies down the hall. His footsteps made no noise. Lace heard Maeve excuse the slaves behind them.

The halls were decorated with tapestries. The designs were intricate and the colors bright. They turned left at the end of the hall and came to a split staircase. Gods, this house was huge.

They approached a rich dark wood double doorway and the slave slowed. Then Lace turned to Delia, taking a deep breath. "Any questions you think I should ask?"

"Ask when the last time he spoke to King James," Delia said.

Lace nodded and logged the question away, and then remembered a question she needed to ask the steward.

She turned to Kylar. "Is this her normal bathing time?"

Kylar nodded. No lie.

"Do you have any questions for me that I could ask your master?" Lace asked.

Kylar's aura brightened with curiosity. He was longing to know Lace's angle in all this. The man shook his head silently.

"I have one question for you, then."

Kylar raised his eyebrows.

"Did Sylvia usually bring a knife with her to the bathing room?"

Kylar nodded. "Always."

"Did it have a snake on one side and a butterfly on the other?"

Kylar shook her head. "It's no snake," he said in a low, raspy voice. "That's a caterpillar."

Ah, so she was stabbed with her own blade.

Lace faced the door. She thought of her first question and the atmosphere she wanted to create. This wouldn't be the first interrogation she'd ever performed, as a soldier in Zoto's army she'd performed many, but this still felt new. She was not in her own territory.

For a moment, she just wished that it were Raj, not Delia who was at her right hand. He was the one who, with a very look, could send peace to her.

She shook herself out of that thought. This wasn't about her. Or Delia. Or Raj. It was about justice for the dead woman and protecting their rebellion. So she set her jaw and opened the door.

The library was vast—two stories of shelves with ladders and stairs leading to them. Leather bound books of all colors and sizes lined the room. For a moment her eyes roved around it in wonder, for she'd never seen as many books in one place. This trove was priceless!

Stim was by the window, looking out into the gardens. His eyes were glazed over, as if he couldn't see the manicured shrubs and bright flowers. The aura surrounding him was steeped in mourning . . . agony, almost.

A middle-aged man who looked like an identical, but younger, version of Stim sat on a couch with a little girl on his lap. His aura was dark and muddled—hard to read. Some auras were misty like his, when people didn't know who they were their auras were clouded. His intelligence was bright, but nothing else was. Almost like his knowledge was the only thing about him.

A pregnant woman sat beside him, staring off into space. She was in shock. Who were they? His children, perhaps?

She quickly scanned each of their clothes but didn't discover any carved bone buttons, missing or present.

Before she spoke, Delia shoved past her. What the hell was she—?

"There's only one way this is going to go," Delia said in a forceful tone. With a mask over her face and her blue eyes glowing with anger, she looked like a nightmare. "If you don't answer all the questions Lace asks you, then we won't protect you. When the rest of the Centurions get here they won't torture *you* for information—they'll torture that child in front of you as you tell them everything, and after your children are dead they won't stop. They'll cut you in tiny bits and throw you across the city." The air seemed to be sucked out of the room. But she went on. "Then they'll kill every slave in the house, slaughter half the city, and invite a new hierarch to take over. If you don't answer Lace right now your lives will slowly end in the worst way imaginable. Anyone who kills a hierarch is a traitor, no matter the circumstance, and King James does NOT SUFFER TRAITORS."

Chapter Twenty-One
Lies and Lichen

Everyone stared at Delia as the prophecies of doom sunk in. The pregnant woman stared up, open mouthed, and the man next to her looked as if all the color had been bleached from his face. The little girl was too young to know what was going on, and continued playing with the toy horse.

Though Delia's threats were directly disobeying Bahir's orders, Lace was strangely relieved by them. The queen had set the mood and given them a glimpse of how serious this was, in case they doubted it—she'd also beamed the spotlight back on Lace.

If she hadn't have been in character, she'd have thanked Delia profusely. Instead, she set her jaw in a hard line and steeled her eyes.

Lace stepped up as if that introduction had been

purposeful. For a second it looked like Delia wasn't going to back down, but then she finally took a step backwards and let Lace fill in the spot.

"We know that," Stim said softly, staring hard at the back of his family's heads. "The only person more dangerous than Bahir is King James. And he's coming for us. We *need* to run. Please, let us out."

The man on the couch jerked as if he'd been hit. "What do you mean, run?" he asked.

Stim looked from Lace to his son. "We have to escape."

"Why?" The man set the toddler on his wife's lap and stood up to face his father. "Just because your wife is dead?"

So Willow was not his mother? That was interesting. Lace didn't cut in—she wanted to know what they'd say next.

"Just hand over Sylvia to King James," the man said. "He can deal with her, and you can continue on as hierarch."

Stim shot across the living room to stand right in front of his son. He peered deep in his eyes. "Everything is gone, Jon. Everything! Since Willow is dead then *we* are dead to King James—and the next Hierarch he puts in charge will likely kill us to keep his reign safe."

"But this is our home." Jon still kept his voice low, probably out of concern for his daughter, but his aura was growing more panicked by the moment.

"Not anymore. Gods, Jon . . . don't you know anything

about your life? Your head has always been trapped in your university work; you've no idea what the world is like."

Lace's eyebrows creased in sympathy when she saw Jon's distress. His expression fell from shock to concern to great fear. He was losing everything in this moment. In contrast, the woman on the couch acted removed from it all. As if she couldn't even hear what was going on. Her eyes followed the speaker but didn't register that she was listening.

"But, we can't leave. Missy isn't feeling well today." He touched the toddler's curls with the tip of his fingers. "She has a cough. And Mary's so late in her pregnancy there's no way she can travel."

The words fell flat in the empty room.

Everything was out of everyone's control right now, and the fact that the little girl had a cough made Lace want to tell him he was lucky that that's the biggest thing he was worried about.

Stim clenched and unclenched his fist, and then sat down on a reading chair. His back was so stiff it looked like a fencepost held him up. Jon collapsed on the couch. He pulled his chin down and hunched his shoulders—his aura was frighteningly dark, as if he might explode in a violent action any moment.

She better walk on eggshells.

Lace cleared her throat. "I'm going to start with a simple question. What is your relation to the Hierarch?"

Stim closed his eyes, in pain. "She is—I mean, she *was* my wife."

Jon looked down and muttered, "My stepmother."

"Where is your real mother?" Delia said.

Another interruption. Lace shot Delia a glare but she pretended to ignore it.

"Dead," Jon said. "Died of lung sickness when I was young."

The woman didn't respond, and Jon patted her hand. "This is my wife, Mary. And our little daughter." Those words were true—and mellowed his aura.

"How long have you been married?" she asked Stim.

"For twelve years." The grief was evident in his voice. Hm, Professor Bahir had been gone from King James' court for twelve years as well.

The little girl crawled off the couch and started playing with the horse on the thick rug. She made neighing sounds and galloped it around the legs of a table.

"Where were you all last night?" she asked. The question hung in the room, reflecting like a sharp beam.

"I was asleep," Stim said dully. "With my wife. She woke up before me, like she always does, to bathe and hear her morning reports. That was the last time I saw her." He appeared to be speaking the truth.

"When were you alerted to her death?" Lace asked. She felt zoned in and focused, aware of nothing but the auras of the suspects and trying to remember every detail.

"Mary woke me and told me." His voice choked. "I couldn't believe it until I saw . . ." he faded away. "Now I'd give anything to unsee . . ."

"Who do you think killed her?" Lace asked pointedly.

Stim paused and gripped the edge of the chair. "Sylvia," he said. But his aura split at the lie. But if he didn't believe it, who else could it be?

The sun broke through the clouds and beams shot through the stained glass windows. Bright colors danced on the marble floor. Oranges and blues and greens. The little girl squealed and raced to them, twirling and rolling in their light.

"What about you two?" she asked Jon and Mary.

Mary leaned her head against his shoulder and he put his arm around her. His aura was still bright with distress, but he wasn't expressing it.

She spoke in an apathetic tone. "I haven't been sleeping well, this late in the pregnancy I never do. But I think—I think—yeah, last night I did. Slept well. That's where I was. In bed. All night." Her words were breathy and her voice wavered.

"Does Jon sleep with you?" Lace asked.

The couple nodded.

"Then what happened this morning?" Lace clasped her hands behind her back and tried to keep her tone and expression even. Neutral. Safe.

"I woke up feeling so groggy." Mary's voice was so dull and sleepy that the words slurred. "So I got up to take a morning stroll with my daughter before breakfast. The garden is so lovely as the sun comes up, you know? So I went straight to the bathing room, first, as I always do, and Willow is usually finished." Her face remained passive. "I saw Willow dead. And I knew that I wouldn't be able to go on a walk anymore. Then I told Stim, and I screamed. He'd know what to do, and I didn't want the slaves to touch her." She slowly closed her eyes, as if falling asleep.

"Mary?" Stim said.

She didn't open her eyes. He frowned. Jon put his arm across her shoulder and squeezed.

"Mary?" Stim said again. "Are you feeling all right?"

She jerked up, blinking her eyes, looking dimly around. "Oh, pardon me. I must have dozed off."

Her aura was as cool and steady as a river, with no emotions to speak of. Lace had seen auras kind of like this before, in people who were severely depressed or had mental illnesses related to trauma. Their minds shut down to protect themselves from what they'd seen. But those auras were still a bit different than this. This was shallower—as if there were emotions below the surface wanting to push out.

But something held them back.

Whatever it was, Lace was suspicious.

"Was Jon in bed when you came downstairs?" Lace asked

Mary nodded.

"I didn't wake until I heard my father's cries," said Jon, speaking softly. His aura split—emotions and thoughts torn by saying something that didn't happen—perhaps not quite a lie, but not the whole truth.

"Were you in bed all night?" she asked.

"No," he said. Truth. "I got up and had my manservant get me a cup of cold goat's milk. I read a little as I waited for him to prepare it, then I drank it and went back to sleep."

"Do you often have sudden urges for milk in the middle of the night?" Arif asked.

"Yes," Jon said. Lace needed to find someone to verify his words.

"When was that?" Lace asked.

Jon shrugged. "Middle of the night." Lie.

"Did you see or hear anything odd?"

"No." Truth.

The little girl stopped playing and stood up, clutching

the horse to her chest. "Ma?" she called, then ran to Stim's knees. "Ma? Horsey?" Her big eyes were round, questioning.

It was so quiet that the flickering candle flame was the only sound. Stim ran his hand over her wispy baby hair. He was so overcome with emotion he couldn't speak.

"Ma's asleep," Jon said in a raspy voice. For the first time there was a flash of sadness in his aura.

Mary leaned her head back on the couch and closed her eyes.

Time was running out. It was almost time to meet Bahir. But these questions had just led to more questions. She mentally shuffled through what she needed to know, and landed on a few last questions that would hopefully cover the most ground.

"Why would Sylvia want to kill Willow?" Lace asked.

He glanced at Kylar, the steward. "Sylvia's children were sold a few months ago and she's never forgiven us for it. When Willow started selling slaves, almost everyone lost someone. They don't say anything, of course, but they all hate her."

"Who else would want to kill her?" Lace asked.

Jon snorted, scornful. "The list is too long to name. Those villagers are getting more riotous by the day—"

Stim broke in, "Couldn't be them. My first thought was that King James finally did what he threatened to do for the past few years—take her out."

It sounded like something King James would do, though: send an assassin to murder a Hierarch and then punish the town for the murder.

"Who else?" Lace pressed.

"No one," Stim said, frustrated. "No one! All the other hierarchs respected her. Everyone in the capitol loved her. And the village. It was rough, but they still respected her. She revolutionized the life for these villagers and they worshipped her for it. Turned them from scaddy fishermen to rich wine merchants and they treated her like a goddess."

Jon scoffed.

Stim must not have been to the town lately, because whatever rich village he was talking about, Seagrove wasn't it. It was obvious he had blinders on his eyes.

"Do you know the families of the men she executed?" Lace asked.

Stim frowned. "They're villagers." He responded as if she'd just asked him to name one of the ants crawling on the ground.

Before she left she remembered one more thing.

"When was the last time Willow heard from King James?"

Stim put his hands on his head. His shoulders bowed and a great trembling fear overtook his aura. "It was a messenger from the capitol informing us that since we weren't enlisted for the upcoming war there'd be a deeper war tax on us. Even if we'd sold everything, which is what Willow wanted, we wouldn't have been able to pay it."

Lace narrowed her eyes. "Does King James know how broke you are?"

"Does it matter?" Stim asked. "She wrote him back a letter begging for an extension while we figured out how to raise the money for the tax. But you know the King . . . he'd take a pound of flesh for a pound of gold if we didn't have it."

Interesting.

Was Willow Stim the pound of flesh?

Chapter Twenty-Two
Rough Skies

Before they left, Lace instructed him to write out the papers of emancipation. He complied right away, saying that the slaves suffering at King James' hands was the last thing he wanted. It gave her a modicum of respect for him.

Delia transformed the glass windows into solid brick walls and changed the door into metal. There'd be no leaving that room until Delia changed it back.

They walked down the stairs and towards the front of the house, leaving the steward behind to guard the door. Lace was deep in thought, mulling over what was said versus the reaction of the auras. They were all lying about one thing or another. But did any of the lies have something to do with the murder?

"In a little while I can send someone to deliver food and

drink and anything else the child may need," Delia said. "The poor thing shouldn't have to suffer."

Arif gasped.

"What?" Delia looked around.

"I didn't know you had a heart," Arif said.

She smirked and smacked him on the arm, then looked a little embarrassed and changed the subject. "Did that woman Mary seem off to you?"

Arif nodded.

"Very," Lace agreed.

"Was she hiding something?" Delia asked Lace, which was the first time she'd ever acknowledged Lace's abilities. Lace appreciated it.

"No," Lace said. "That's what was odd. She's a shallow lady, but something was holding her back today. I can't read what it was in her aura."

"She's just in shock," Arif said. "She saw her dead mother-in-law. That would disturb anyone."

Lace knew it was more than that. If it were trauma, the aura would be more complicated. Overwhelming stress, pain, and gripping fright manifesting in numbness and disconnection. Like Stim's. But this one was bland.

They walked down the silent, empty halls. Ghosts of light trickled through the curtained windows. Rich carpets, gorgeous statues of people and animals, and carvings. If they had more time Lace would have loved to look at all the architecture and pore over the paintings and sculptures—she adored art but wasn't exposed to it very often.

In Zoto their art was weaving—cloth, baskets, and stories. And the music—the music was masterful and developed and the musicians heavily trained and respected and well paid. This art was so different than what she'd seen, she wished she could explore it.

"Is this what King James' palace looks like?" Lace asked, imagining that nothing could be much more expensive or fine than this. Vases full of white lilies freshened the air with their scent and there was something beautiful to look at anywhere the eye landed.

Delia looked around and her expression darkened. "Picture this, only twenty times bigger, richer, more slaves, guards, and weapons, and everyone was fifty times more scared. That's King James' castle."

A wave of compassion rolled over Lace. That was what Delia had to live in, a gilded cage. A façade of power. A puppet slave.

"I'm sensing you don't crave your old home," Lace said.

"Don't need a gift to see that," Arif said.

"I want to see everything burn," Delia said.

"Everything?" Lace raised her eyebrows.

"Everything," Delia said, then paused. "Except the

orchard. There are some magnificent cherry trees."

**

The butterfly garden had a glass ceiling that filtered in the light. A stonework trail led through a maze of tall bushes and small trees, bright flowers flooded the ground like a colorful river. The sound of gurgling water filled the garden.

Lace's breath caught.

Hundreds of butterflies flitted from one bud to the next. She'd never seen such an array of them. Every color, every size. With each flap of their wings they jumped through the air, impossibly fast, then went stone still as they drank nectar from the flowers.

The group was in the middle of the garden, sitting on benches. A tiny pond with a trickling fountain at the center was in the middle.

Lace grinned when she saw Violet. The woman was completely covered in butterflies. They were on her hair, her nose, her shoulders, and covered her lap. She had a worshipful, rapt expression on her face, and her aura was so light and joyous it lifted Lace to see.

Little sounds escaped Violet, as if she were talking to a baby.

Then her eyes caught Arif. He had a bright blue butterfly on his shoulder, which he was studying intently. His aura flared with curiosity and pleasure.

Cannon came up to Delia, put his arm around her, and gave her a quiet kiss on her hair. She melted into his side. Then he brought her chin up and gave her a deep kiss. Their love was sweet to see, in the midst of all this death.

Raj looked across the garden's window to the town—his aura was dark and brooding. With soft steps she came up behind him. "What troubles you?"

He turned, stony faced as usual, but the sun caught in his eyes and made them glow. His aura turned from dark blue to a sunny bright, just from seeing her. Her lips parted in pleasure at the change in him. He brushed his hair back. All she saw were his eyes, hungry, longing, and yet content at the sight of her.

Raj was about to speak when Professor Bahir called the group together. Regretfully, Lace turned and formed a circle with the students.

"Tell me a fact that you know about this murder," Professor Bahir said.

Violet was bouncing on the balls of her feet she was so excited. Her frizzy hair bounced around her face. The moment Bahir stopped talking she said, "Ferns!"

Everyone stared at her.

"You like ferns?" Lace said, laughter behind her voice.

"Very much," Violet said.

"Do ferns have anything to do with the murder?" Bahir

asked patiently.

"YES!" she shouted and gripped his arm. "I found spores on the collar of Willow's gown. And some on the ground in front of her. And even some in the hallway, near the front door."

"What does that mean, Violet?" Bahir asked.

"It means that the murderer was near ferns and dropped spores all over the place. And guess what?" Violet clapped her hands and smiled. "There are no ferns in this property!"

But how could someone have gotten past the front gate? That'd be quite a feat.

"Good work, my dear," Bahir said. "Next?"

Delia took a deep breath. "During the interrogation with the family it seems as if Stim is deluded as to what the town is going through. He spoke about her being a goddess and a savior . . ." she faded off and gestured towards the town. "And the Hierarch also said that King James issued a war tax on them since they didn't join as soldiers, and there's no way they can pay it." Her cheeks flushed. "That gives the king a reason to send an assassin to murder Hierarch Willow."

"Good info." Bahir nodded. "Arif? What are you thinking?"

He trilled his fingers in the air and looked up. His lithe, tattooed body was taut and he looked out to the sea as if it called his name. "I'm thinking of the air."

"Aye?" Bahir said. "You're thinking of the air and Violet's thinking of ferns. My naturalists have a one track mind."

The students smiled.

"Listen, listen, listen," Arif said and when he clenched his fists a powerful gust of wind whipped over them. Lace's hair caught and tickled her neck, falling into her eyes so she held it back with her hand. He leaned forward and weaved his fingers through the air. "We're running out of time—the Centurions are probably already flying here from the capitol. If I distress the air, spike the winds, thicken the clouds, give some bite to the skies, then the Centurions won't have a straight shot from the capitol." He laughed. "I'll throw them on their backs and drive them into the sea."

Everyone nodded at the thought.

Professor Bahir grew serious. "At the very least it'd make them teleport through another magnetic trail, besides ours, and that will deplete their magic. Excellent idea, son. Do it. Raj?"

Raj clenched his jaw and remained stony faced. What was he waiting for? His aura was nervous. She gave him an encouraging smile. A light came back into his eyes. "I-I want to see what the town says about the Hierarch's murder—hear what it is like under her rule. Even if it ends up having nothing to do with the murder I believe it will help us in the rebellion to know the thoughts of the town."

Professor Bahir nodded. "Big thinking. Thank you. Now Lace, what did you learn during the interrogation?"

Lace sorted through which bite she should feed first. She took a moment to gather her thoughts, then said, "Everyone is lying. Stim lied about believing Sylvia is the murderer, I think he knows more than he's telling. Something strange, though not magical, is happening with the daughter-in-law. And Stim's son, Jon, has no love for his stepmother and he got up in the night and did something he lied about." Then she made eye contact with Bahir. "And they sold Sylvia's children to the King's quarries, which is *unforgivable*." She said the word with vehemence. "And Stim really hates you."

Bahir ignored that last statement. "And has no one has found the owner to the button?" Bahir asked.

Everyone shook their heads.

Cannon cleared his throat. "Well, when we spoke to Sylvia she said she'd murdered Willow. After her children were sold she still had hope that Willow would buy them back, but when Willow executed the villagers she decided to take justice into her own hand."

"So is that it?" Raj asked. "They caught the murderer red handed and so we collect all the information she may have left about the rebellion and deliver her to—"

Cannon interrupted. "She was caught with the knife,

which didn't kill Willow."

"But she confessed!" Delia said. "And the Centurions may spare the town if they've caught the murderer."

Lace shook her head frantically. Her stomach clenched in a knot. Sylvia was lying, she hadn't murdered Willow—and though she may be noble enough to sacrifice herself for the town, there was no way Lace would let it get to that point. She looked with apprehension at Professor Bahir, gauging his thoughts.

"Sylvia is the most likely murderer—" Lace opened her mouth to protest and he held up his hand. "But, because of Lace's knowledge of her lie, we must prove it beyond a doubt. We still have much work to do."

Chapter Twenty-Three
Past Never Leaves

Professor Bahir still looked weak, though his magic had risen. Arif was still playing his fingers through the wind and he couldn't stop looking towards the sea.

Bahir spoke quickly, "Now we have to search the house for any information Willow may have had regarding her relationship with the rebellion. It must be clear before we leave. Raj, you help me with that. Anything with a harp sign on it will be notable, that's the sign of our rebellion."

"A harp? Why?" Lace asked.

Bahir shrugged. "It just became that. I'm not sure why. It didn't start with me."

Lace turned from the group and took in the garden. She took a deep breath. It smelled like honey and rich rose-scent and dark earth. On almost every surface was a butterfly.

When she was young she loved catching them in a net. Her sister would pin the ones she found onto a board, but Lace always freed hers. She felt like they were bits of flowers' souls flittering through the air.

"We've got to get moving." Bahir straightened. "Arif, you form a storm to keep the Centurions at bay. Cannon, you devise a plan on how to rescue everyone from this home before the Centurions arrive. And Lace, Violet, and Delia, you go find the ferns."

Oh scad. Fern duty. With miss priss.

"And Lace . . ." Professor Bahir said. "Don't forget about your mission."

What the hell, why would he single her out like that, of course she wouldn't forget the mission how could he—wait . . . at his expression, she suddenly remembered what he meant. It wasn't about the murder. He was talking about befriending Delia.

Well, Delia hadn't been so bad lately. In fact, Lace had gained a level of respect for Delia over the past few hours. There was a gleam of hope that perhaps, somehow, they might be able to be friends.

But if she didn't succeed, it wouldn't be her fault. She gave a slight bow to Professor.

"The town is dangerous," Arif objected. "Why send the girls—" He cut himself off at the disgusted looks sent his way.

"How about I transform your lips into a lizard?" Delia said.

"Or fill your underwear with stinging nettles?" Violet said.

Lace flicked him the rude finger and turned away. "We can handle ourselves."

As she walked across the garden Raj went after her and took her arm, whispering in her ear. "I know you can handle yourself."

She knew that too.

"Just don't let Delia handle you," he said pointedly. "You're every bit as good as she is."

Lace knew that too. But still, it warmed her heart to hear it from voices other than the one in her head.

Chapter Twenty-Four
Stone's Throw

The gate was unlocked by the guard and the three ladies made their way into the village. Their red uniforms looked sharp and bright in the dull streets—they were the only ones out—their black, red, and blonde hair bobbed in the wind. Lace sped up, going past the decaying bodies swinging on the gallows.

Pressing a handkerchief to her nose, she eyed the town.

"Are we just going to comb through the streets looking for ferns?" Delia said, obviously frustrated at her assigned mission.

Violet cocked her eyebrows. "I don't need a comb. I can smell them."

The roads were empty. Their pants rustled as they walked. Stray cats surveyed them from atop fences and roofs.

She felt eyes on her, and auras clouded behind walls and windows. They were dark, afraid.

"Lead the way," Lace said.

Violet sniffed and turned down a small street. "These spores smell like Dakinian Ferns, if I'm not mistaken."

"That's amazing," Delia said.

"Aye." Lace nodded. "I can't even smell the difference between plums and strawberries."

Violet grinned.

Lace kept a wary eye out for any approaching auras or threatening forms. With all the upheaval the village had been through, there's no knowing what they'd do to invading Centurions.

As they walked she went through all the murder details in her mind and came up with some questions she'd ask once they caught the person who'd crept into the house. "What I don't understand is how the person got over the fence and into the house without anyone seeing them."

"It's quite a feat," Delia said. "Those guards look experienced, and that wall is tall."

"Where is everyone?" Violet broke out. "I wonder if people have already been evacuating?"

"Maybe those who have a place to go, and enough money to get there" Lace said.

"Not everyone has the luxury of being able to leave,"

Delia said.

Halfway down the street Lace heard the sound of sizzling and the unmistakable smell of breaded cheese balls. Her mouth watered. It'd been a long time since supper last night. Violet cut straight to the store where the smell came from.

Large glass windows revealed people milling about inside, eating fried cheese on sticks and talking in low voices. Their clothes were old and worn, but clean.

When they saw the ladies they froze, staring wide eyed as if they were fish stuck in a bowl.

"Maybe it wasn't ferns you're smelling—" Delia said dryly. "It's cheese."

"Mmm," Violet said. "Fried cheese. Anyone have any money?"

Lace shook her head. "I didn't know this was going to be a shopping trip."

"Centurions don't pay—they take." Delia said.

"What?" Lace snapped. "We don't have time for this. We should be looking for ferns."

"No!" Delia insisted. "We need to get a grasp of the town's reaction. No place better than where people are gathering." She sniffed, then walked into the store front.

With an internal groan, Lace followed her.

The crowd backed away from her as she made her way

to the counter. Lace followed with tentative steps, wary of a violent outburst. Though most of the people's auras were frightened, a few were bristling in anger.

"I'll take three," Delia said sharply to the woman, and was handed the breaded, steaming cheese on a stick. "And wine," Delia added. She turned to Lace and Violet. "Want a glass?"

They shook their heads. Lace felt pinched and uncomfortable about stealing the food, but it's exactly what the apprentices would've done.

The people stared at Violet, though Lace could tell they tried not to. She looked so naked next to their gray and brown conservative attire. Where the women all had scarves over their heads, all she had was a scarf wrapped around her hips and necklaces covering her breasts. Whether conscious or not, Violet flipped her hair over her shoulders and a few of the women gasped—a mother covered her son's eyes. It made Violet smile so wide her cheeks dimpled. She really didn't give a scad.

Lace thought Violet had never looked prettier. As if she were a lone bright flower in a heap of brown earth.

Violet took a much-too-large bite into a cheese ball with a contented sigh, then munched with her mouth open. Delia just held hers—she couldn't eat with the mask in place.

The smell was delicious and Lace couldn't wait a second

longer. She bit into the crispy shell. The cheese was hot—she breathed out sharply to cool it on her tongue, then swallowed it. Salty and creamy, with a hint of garlic. Perfection. She ate up the rest of the cheese balls in two bites.

After chewing quickly and swallowing, Violet said, "Know where any ferns are, people?"

Almost in unison, everyone shook his or her head no.

"Anyone see someone sneak into the Hierarch's house last night?" Lace asked.

They either shook their heads or silently glared. It didn't matter what the question was. They weren't going to talk.

"How can you not know where the ferns are?" Violet scolded.

"Ah," Delia said in a sarcastic tone. "You must all be new to the town."

The cheese seller nodded.

Delia lifted her mask slightly and put the wine to her lips, gulping down the burgundy liquid. Lace could smell the fruity, aromatic scent from where she stood.

Delia clenched the wine glass and then smashed it on the ground. It shattered, skittering glass everywhere in the room. Violet jumped. A splinter hit Lace's ankle. That was one way to get the people's attention.

People pulled away from her in fear.

"Listen! Someone from town was in the Hierarch's

palace last night," Delia said. "We're here to find who that is. Perhaps your tongues won't be cut out and your eyes removed from their sockets if we find who the culprit is before the Centurions arrive. They will *not* be merciful."

The people stepped back and a woman clutched her little toddler to her. Their faces froze in fear, the men's faces wrinkled in anger and loathing. Gods, Delia. She knew how to throw a threat around, didn't she?

"Has anyone heard any hate speech against the Hierarch?" Lace asked.

No one responded.

"Of course not," Delia said. Her voice was sharp and angry, though her aura was calm and confident. She must be baiting them so that Lace could read their auras. Marvelous, really. "Then can anyone tell me who would want to kill the Hierarch?"

An old man stepped forward. Judging from his wrinkles he looked to be about a thousand. He leaned on a crutch and had a long braid down his back. The older woman next to him tugged his arm back but he didn't budge. He had the type of aura that was steady as the tide. "The Hierarch was good to us," he ascended his head, "as King James is. Blessings on his head. We are thankful for their care and mourn the Hierarch's death."

"Murder!" Delia said sharply. Her eyes flashed.

"Someone from this town crept through the gates and plunged a knife in your dear leader's heart. If that doesn't set your town afire with fear, then you are more foolish than I give you credit for. You should be shoving the culprit at us."

The people wouldn't make eye contact with her—they shifted from foot to foot, wary. Violet took another bite that was too big for her mouth. She chomped on the cheese and stared, entranced, at Delia.

"You will all die in horrible ways if you won't—"

Lace broke in, "If you will not tell us anything then at least tell us this, who are the men swinging from the gallows?"

The old woman beside the man bowed her head. "A father and his son."

"And *what* are their names?" Delia's voice rang out.

The old man swallowed. "Kinkades. Christian and Stephen Kinkade."

A young man, handsome and red faced, slammed his hand down on the table he sat at. He stood up, the chair scraped against the floor. Lace's skin prickled with tension— he wanted a fight.

Oh, but he was far, far outmatched.

"You don't want to do that," she told him in a low voice. Then Delia drew her knife and Lace grabbed her forearm.

"Curses be on the Hierarch's head and curses be on King

James' head," he said. The people gasped and the old man charged at him. He spoke quickly. "We are slaves. He takes everything from us—"

The old man slapped the young man in the face. The hit resounded. His head snapped back and a welt appeared on his cheek.

The young man's eyes glistened with passion and hurt. The old man turned and bowed on his knees before the ladies. "Please forgive—oh, please forgive such a fool. Take my life if you must . . ." He grabbed the young man's wrist and wrenched him to his knees. Everyone followed, trembling in fear. A child whimpered, then started wailing.

Lace's heart ached to see the terror and loathing in the villagers. They were trapped under a cruel rule, and no matter how much Willow cared for them or protected them, she was still the arm of King James. They were slowly bleeding out and there was nothing they could do about it.

"But where are the ferns?" Violet said in a bright voice. "Perhaps east of the village. Ferns love being east of things." She rubbed her oily hands on her curly hair and then sauntered out of the store.

Lace wished she could transport everyone to Zoto, or at least to Moth Valley. Things would not go well for them once the Centurions came and the rebellion and missing taxes were discovered. They'd be refugees, fleeing across the border soon. The storm was coming.

Delia leaned toward the old man as she backed out of the store. "Keep that young man muzzled when the Centurions get here, unless you want to get salted."

Salted was a term the Drams used for when King James decimated a town—it became as useless as salted soil.

The old woman stood up straight. She brought her scarf over her mouth and looked down. "But this is our home. Those vines are our children. We can't transplant them."

Lace shook her head sadly and walked out.

Chapter Twenty-Five
Delia's Teaching

When Lace stepped outside the shop, tumultuous clouds fought the eastern horizon. Sharp, cold wind gusted in from the sea, smelling of brine and fish. The dark sky loomed towards them. The wind bit through her jacket, and she buttoned the top button, shivering. Lightning cracked and then a few seconds later thunder rumbled, so loud the rocks jostled.

"Let's go east," Violet said.

They walked down the empty road. The wind whipped their hair back and forth in their faces.

"You were marvelous in there," Lace said to Delia, and she really meant it.

"Was I?" Delia frowned and pushed her glossy hair behind her ear. "I just wanted them to know what a dire situation they were in."

"You made that clear," Lace said.

"Good." Delia nodded. "I only want to protect them."

What the villagers needed wasn't gentle questions or polite urgings, which is what Lace would've done if she had led that conversation. What they needed was the living scad scared out of them. Like Bahir said, there wasn't just one way to protect people from evil.

Thunder rumbled. Then lightning shot across the sky. They walked in silence down the road.

"Arif is having a good time," Delia said. She moved her mask away and took a bite out of the cold cheese ball she'd been carrying.

"Those were so good. I could eat like a dozen more of those cheese balls," Lace said.

Delia took one off of the stick and handed it to her.

"Oh, Gods." Lace held her hands up. "I don't want yours, I didn't mean—"

"I know you didn't," Delia said, earnest. "But really, I don't want it." Her aura split—it was a half-truth.

"If Lace doesn't eat it, I will," Violet piped up. Lace chuckled, then grudgingly took it from Delia. She split it in half and popped half in her mouth and gave the rest to Violet.

Lace studied the clouds. They were dark gray, and

tinged with purple. The sun was trying to burst through, which added a ghostly glow to them.

"That deep feeling in the pit of my insides before a storm . . ." Violet said. "Mmm, it's delicious."

"I like it, too," Lace said. "It energizes and relaxes me at the same moment, like I should either fly to the stars or take a nap."

The air brimmed with charged static.

"I know what you mean," Violet exclaimed. "My magic is stronger during storms."

"Mine, too!" Lace's eyes lit. "It's like something gets trapped under my skin and it builds up like a thirst, and if I don't use my magic I might—"

"Dry up," Violet finished for her. "I know! And the moment my magic starts spinning out of me I get a rushing release, as if all my thirst was quenched."

"And . . ." Lace couldn't talk fast enough, having never shared these feelings with someone before. "Do you feel connected to the earth somehow? Like you're caught in the flow of a stream, or destiny, and . . . I don't know, tapped into a greater power? I feel like I am in the earth's aura."

"Gods, yes!" Violet's green eyes shone. "I feel wrapped in Mama Earth's arms, protected and infinitely powerful."

To speak like this and have someone hear her was a thrill. A laugh bubbled out of her she was so happy to share this. "No one else has ever understood what I mean when I say I wanted to jump into the heart of a storm."

"I have no idea what you mean," Delia said, lifting her chin.

Some of the excitement drained from Lace's face.

"Well, that's understandable. Your magic is more formulaic, like Cannon and Raj's. Your skills are more dependable," Lace said. "Ours is instinctual."

"Wild," Delia said.

"Yes!" Violet skipped.

"But I—" Delia began, then stopped herself. "I feel the opposite during storms. I've always been scared—no, not scared . . . nervous of them," she amended. "When I was little I hid under my covers in bed until they were gone." Her aura split. She probably *still* hid under the covers during storms.

"Are you nervous now?" Lace asked.

Delia nodded. "Having storm magic-power would be nice."

"I think it'd be *nice* to transform my bread into bread pudding any time I wanted, like you can," Violet said.

Delia grinned, then sighed and her shoulders relaxed in relief.

Seagulls looped overhead. Their incessant calls filled the city. They took a few turns and the buildings went from stores to houses. Somewhere, a baby cried.

"I hate seaports," Delia said. "There's nothing more annoying than a seagull's call."

"I can think of something," Lace said.

Delia looked over.

"The only thing more annoying than a seagull's call is *hundreds* of seagulls calling."

Delia snorted.

"I like the sound," Violet said. "They're just really communicative birds and they always have a lot to say to each other. It helps them work and play and mate a lot easier than other species of birds, because they call so often."

"Still annoying," Lace and Delia said at the same time.

Another streak of lightning lit the sky. The clouds had gathered and completely blocked the sun; everything grew chill.

Suddenly, Delia hurried over, an intent look in her eye. She brushed a strand of blond hair behind her ear. "Let me tell you something," Delia said, coming closer. And closer. "It's a secret," she said. Stopping right at her shoulder, Delia lifted her hand to cover the side of her mouth and she whispered in Lace's ear.

"I want to teach you the secret to carrying more than one person in the air," she said.

Lace just stared, confused.

"We aren't people." Her warm breath tickled Lace's ear.

"We are just seven pockets of air. You can hold seven pockets of air, can't you?"

Lace hesitated, then nodded. Yes. Holding pockets of air was easy—but . . . "How can the pockets hold everyone? Aren't they too weak?"

"No," Delia whispered. "Whether it's a boat or a person or a paper, the air holds them the same."

"Delia!" Lace leaned back, suddenly aware of what she was saying. "Why are you whispering? And how do you know all this about auras?"

Delia looked deep into Lace's eyes, searching. Her blue eyes were bright and intense, her chubby cheek tinged pink. She was on the brink of telling a secret.

"Really, tell me," Lace said.

"Don't tell anyone," Delia whispered. "Promise?"

"I promise," Lace whispered back, expecting the worst.

Delia swallowed, then leaned forward and whispered. Lace smelled the fear in her words. "King James is an aura reader, just like you."

Lace gasped, covering her mouth with her hand. She never knew! He'd always professed to being non-magical. He'd never shown his power before!

"And-and—" Delia stuttered.

"And what?"

"And I'm the one who trained him!"

She was still too stunned to respond. No wonder Delia had faced her with such caution and distrust. The only aura reader she'd ever been around was hateful.

It was too much to sink in at the moment, she held it out as if guarding herself from it—she'd have to deal with it later.

They walked past the shops and tradesmiths and came into a part of town that was mostly houses. A few little park-areas were set up with game nets and tended flowers and marble statues from Dram's mythos—like Mauriel the Goddess who controlled the sea, and Pagon the half-man, half-fish who created storms.

Violet sniffed the air. "I smell a spore," she said in a light voice. "We're getting close to the murderer."

"Be quiet then," Delia said, tensing up. "If you *can.*"

They came to a little nook in the road—a statue of an angel surrounded by two columns. Candles were lit, hundreds strong, flickering in vigil. The flames jostled in the wind. Presents and flowers were laid beside the candles. This was some sort of remembrance.

"I think we've come to the right house," Lace said. "This is probably be the Kinkades, and these candles are lit in memory of their father and brother."

An aura hid behind the wall, but was walking quickly towards them. Lace tensed and whispered, "We've got someone approaching."

"The ferns are close," Violet said. "Right over that wall."

Delia hurried her pace. "Let's get this over with. I hate being on the streets."

Two other auras slipped out of houses behind them and started walking down the alley, heading towards them. Then another one to their right crept up, hiding behind a horse cart. Four in all. She had no time to study them, all she knew was that they were mages.

It was illegal for any mages to live outside King James' castle. He either killed them or used them as his slaves. These mages were either spies from another country, servants of King James, or undiscovered. Whoever they were, they'd probably have it out for the Centurions.

"We're getting surrounded," Lace said. "By mages."

Magic flared in Delia's hand. She widened her eyes. "Where?"

"I can't see them," Lace said. "But they're coming. One behind the wall. Two in the alley. One hiding behind that horse cart."

Suddenly the aura stepped out from behind the fence, and Lace gasped. There was no one attached to it.

Chapter Twenty-Six
The Mages

"Run!" Lace shouted. "They're invisible!"

They took off down the street. Whoever was behind them was in their home territory, and Lace didn't want to fight them head on.

A force field suddenly surrounded them. The sounds of the gulls were muffled. They froze in space. Lace strained her arm but it was trapped in the air.

Remembering one of Professor Bahir's lectures, force fields were usually created by *changers*. And they didn't trap magic—they trapped air. Which meant her magic couldn't be contained.

The force field tightened. It squeezed Lace's chest and she gave a low groan. Violet grunted and struggled and Delia was still. Still and angry. Lace was the only one who could fight the mages because she could see their auras.

"Where are they?" Delia yelled.

"Oy," Lace said through her teeth. "They're at the wall. In the alley. Behind the horse cart."

The force field yanked them down and they smashed into the ground. It pressed Lace's shoulders flat, but her neck was craned and she could still see the street. The force field wavered, releasing for a split second before gripping them again.

Whoever held them was not very experienced.

Delia's hands burst red and the horse cart transformed into blistering flames. Lace felt the heat from where they were. Smoke poured up like a funnel. A child yelped and jumped out from behind it. He had to be no older than twelve, ratty haired and gangly limbed.

At the same time Violet spoke an arcane word. At first Lace thought that nothing had happened, but then birds of all sizes came flying like a feathery cloud. They gathered from all over. At least half of them were pure white seagulls. They dove into the alleyway with a cacophony of shrieks and calls and flapping wings.

Two little girls tore out of the alley, crying out and covering their heads. A burst of birds nipped at their hair and clawed their backs.

Lace concentrated on the aura in front of the wall—it

must be the telepath. She focused on the area, visualizing a body. Then she gripped the air's aura and jerked.

With a cry, a teenage girl appeared. Out of control, she fell on her ass. Her legs flew up over her head and she crashed into the wall. Instantly the force field vanished.

The girl fell, limp, and her head cracked against the stone. Lace felt a jolt of fear. She didn't mean to seriously injure the girl.

In one smooth movement Lace got to her feet, and drew her knife. The three children ran to the teen girl and hovered around her. One gripped her shoulder and urged her to get up, casting fearful glances at the trio of ladies.

The flock of birds fluttered and jumped in the alleyway, waiting for Violet's signal. Their beady eyes glittered in the shadows.

Violet and Delia took Lace's right and left sides. They slowly approached the child mages.

The teenage girl's hair was wavy blonde and cropped above her ears. She had thick eye make up on, pink lips, and wore a simple gray dress. Her aura had a horrific black slithering tear across it. Something dark, traumatic, and life changing had happened to her recently.

The children's eyes were sunken in, as if they hadn't slept or eaten in days. The littlest girl, who looked to be around eight, had sores around her mouth and her hair was gnarled. There were twins with big doe eyes and gentle mouths—they had bruises on their arms and bare, dirty feet.

These were no spies or servants of King James. They weren't even out of school. Might not even be *in* school. They had to be underground mages—kept hidden from the Hierarch so they wouldn't be sent away.

Their body types and facial features were similar; Lace guessed they were all in the same family. Their auras were weak and shaky, trembling in the rain.

They were terrified.

There had to be more to this attack than general vitriol against the King. Lace would bet her last dose of magic that they were hiding something.

Now how could they discover what it was without threatening them?

"Don't hurt the children," Violet said quietly. She combed her hair back with her hand, getting it out of her eyes. Her pink skin shone bright with sweat.

"Of course I won't," Delia snapped. They approached the child mages. The teen girl was just starting to sit up, she rubbed her head and winced. The youngest was crying.

Lace filtered through ideas on how they can get information without harm. "We need to know what they know," Lace began. "How can we—"

"Follow my lead." Delia raised her hands in a dramatic

gesture as if to throw more magic. "By order of King James I—" The kids scrambled back and the teen clapped her hands, capturing them in a force field. Again. Her eyes were wide and startled, as if she didn't know what she was doing; only responding instinctually.

"Delia," Lace muttered through her teeth.

"Let them," Delia said. "Let them have us."

That's right! Scad, it was a good plan. Impressive, on such short notice. If the children thought they'd captured the ladies and had them in control, that'd be the only way for them to relax and get their guard down. "Brilliant," she told Delia. As long as they didn't get murdered.

"They'll take us to the ferns," Violet said in a muffled voice. She said a word and the flock of birds deserted—the sound of flapping wings overcame the alley and with a flurry of feathers they were gone.

"Do you have them?" the boy-twin said. He had dark, curly hair, a scar across his neck, and the same pink lips as his sister.

The teen girl struggled to her feet, breathing heavily and tensing every muscle in her body. "I—I can't hold them for long." She grunted in concentration and her face reddened, as if bearing a great burden.

"Let's tie them before you lose it," the littlest said and took out handfuls of rope from her bag.

"Shhh," said the cautious-faced girl-twin with a leather vest and long skirt. "They can hear us."

Lace didn't look at them; she kept her eyes down.

The littlest approached them, full of innocent tenacity. Her brown curls bounced as she ran.

"Be careful!" the boy shouted and ran after her. "The brownie has a knife." He approached warily, creeping up as if she was going to slice them any moment. Then he roughly pried Lace's fingers open and took the knife.

"I—I—I can't hold much long—" the teen girl groaned.

The quiet twin girl covered her eyes with her hands, overcome with nerves.

The boy's hands shook, but he took the knife with both hands and ran around the bubble of air so he was right behind Lace.

The way the teen girl was acting, so inexperienced and out of practice, it reminded Lace of herself when she was training on her own. Not able to tell if her skills were really great or really bad.

The force field wavered and dropped. All three of them went limp and dropped to their knees, on purpose. Lace tried to give a convincing fall, and staggered a little. The boy grabbed her shoulder and pressed the knife in her back. He was shaking so badly she was afraid he'd cut her jacket. "Don't—don't move, aye? You hear? If you do, I'm going to—I—I will kill you."

Lace swallowed down her smile. He was so unconvincing.

"Don't move," she said to Violet and Delia, "Or he'll kill me." He relaxed a little at her words.

They held up their hands. Lace hoped they wouldn't take off Delia's mask. If they found King James' most wanted criminal they'd know too much.

The youngest girl tied them with her rope. With her tongue sticking out the side of her mouth in concentration, she drew the most complicated and hearty knots Lace had ever seen. In just moments. Lace watched her create them in wonder. She must know a sailor or two who shared their tricks with her.

Quicker than she thought possible, each of them were bound tightly. The only way Lace could get out of it was if Delia turned the rope into noodles or something. Quite impressive.

Behind the fence Lace noticed some greenery and a courtyard, attached to the only house on the block. This family was rich. Or, had once been rich. The children gathered around the three women, staring down at them as if they were strange beings.

The teen girl lifted her chin and puffed out her chest, her eyes took on a haughty glint. If she thought that she could capture three Centurion apprentices with weak magic and one knife then they knew nothing about Centurions or magic.

"Garden, the garden," the quiet girl said, motioning behind the wall. "Before Mother sees."

"Mother won't see, she's in her room, she's *always* in her room," the littlest said.

The teen took Lace's arm and wrenched her up. She stumbled along, following the girl with heavy steps. "Go, or I'll slice you," she heard the boy say behind her.

When they crossed the fence, they closed the gate behind them and locked it.

Time to begin the interrogation.

Chapter Twenty-Seven
Ferns

Dozens of golden and blue butterflies wisped from bloom to bloom, drinking up nectar. A little vegetable garden in the corner was not doing too well. It looked new, hastily planted in shallow soil. The potato vines were riddled with bug bites and the rows of beans were wilted and brown. Whoever was tending it did not have any experience.

"Oh, look!" Violet said in delight. "I love your ferns! I've been looking all over for them."

And there they were. Violet did have a good nose after all.

The side of the garden that led to the back porch of the house was completely covered in ferns. They climbed up the pear tree and up the columns of the porch. In the sunbeams, little spores could be seen floating in the air. It made Lace's nose tickle just to see them.

That meant that someone who lived here might've been to the room where Willow was murdered.

Puzzle pieces were starting to fall in place.

Lace looked over her shoulder to make sure Delia and Violet were following. Just as she did, the oldest girl pushed her in the middle of the back. She tripped over the side of her foot. Instinctually she grabbed the air's aura to catch herself, then realized in time that she shouldn't and braced for impact.

She smashed against the white rock. It bit into her skin, drawing blood on her cheek.

"Pansy!" the littlest girl exclaimed. "Be careful!"

Lace struggled to get to her knees.

"Watch it, girl," Delia said sharply.

"I—I didn't mean—" Pansy began, then stopped. Her eyes hardened. "These bitches deserve anything they get." The siblings looked at their older sister, shocked. She just set her jaw and roughly handled Violet and Delia until they were on their knees in a line. She put her hands on her hips and strode in front of them.

Pansy had the same body type as Delia, and they looked similar. Pure Dram. Both had round, pink faces and voluptuous hips and buxom chests, covered in a layer of softness. Eyes were round and blue, and the only difference was that the teen girl's hair was shorn and Delia's was perfectly twisted and shaped into a formal hairdo, with a few loose tendrils falling around her face.

Pansy looked strong. But strong enough to strangle an adult woman high over her head? That was doubtful. Could she be working with someone in the mansion? Sylvia, maybe?

The motive was there. Willow had stolen people very close to both of them, if indeed these were the Kinkades.

The children turned their backs on the ladies and huddled together, whispering in loud-children-whispers.

"What're we going to do?" the boy said. "I told you she couldn't keep a secret."

"They'll be trapped forever and ever in my knots," the littlest one said.

"Should they be killed too?" the quiet one said with sadness in her voice. Scad, how many people had these kids murdered?

"Be quiet, I need to think!" Pansy said. She bit her lip and tapped her fingers on her hip.

Little robins bounced across the grass, looking for worms. Lace heard trickling water but couldn't see a fountain anywhere.

Finally, Pansy turned to them. "Are there more of you coming?"

Lace nodded.

"Are you the Kinkades?" Delia asked.

The littlest girl's eyes widened. "Can you read minds?" she asked.

"No, you little cuttlefish," Pansy said. "No one can read minds except the gods."

"Don't call me cuttlefish!" the littlest girl said and stamped her foot.

A golden butterfly fluttered from one of the flowers to land on Violet's shoulder. It moved its wings slowly, folding and unfolding them, and Violet gave it a soft smile.

The clouds grew darker and stormier—Arif was still at work driving the Centurions away with his weather. Lightning flashed and lit the garden. Seconds later thunder boomed, and the boy jumped so hard he almost dropped the knife.

"Who are you?" Pansy asked Lace.

"I'm a mage," Lace said. "And I've come to find out who killed Hierarch Willow."

The children paled. The twin girl's hands flew to her mouth. Pansy's eyes reddened and her hands trembled.

"It wasn't me." Pansy leaned forward with earnest, round eyes. But her aura split at the lie. "I've never even been in the mansion."

Violet sniffed. "I followed the ferns. Their scent is so

strong, especially this time of year, when love is in the air and they spore with each other. Someone who lives here was in the mansion."

For the first time it looked as if Pansy was starting to realize that she did not have the upper hand here. She glanced nervously at her siblings, protective of them.

"If you're innocent," Delia said in a measured voice. "Then why did you capture us?"

Lace looked down and spoke to the white gravel ground. "I can imagine how angry you are. Losing your father and—"

"Not just Father!" Pansy said. "My brother too. *My brother*. My best friend."

"I don't think Father is coming back," the littlest one said, voice breaking. "Ever."

At her words, Lace's heart clenched. She knew what it was like to lose a parent before her eyes and she wished with all her might that there were something she could say that would make these children feel better.

But there wasn't.

There was only time. Time would tame some of the anguish of the wound.

She could, however, protect them.

"Are you going to kill them?" the twin girl said in an anguished voice.

"Are they going to kill us?" the littlest wailed.

"I won't let them!" The boy took a threatening step towards him.

"You brought ferns into the Hierarch's palace," Violet said. "No use lying about it. I can smell them. They're the very same you have in your yard. And Lace here is an aura reader so she can tell when you're lying anyway."

They looked at Lace in fearful awe.

"You can turn invisible," Delia said. "So you could go past the gates without anyone witnessing you."

"Your life was shattered by the Hierarch," Lace said. "If there's anyone who you'd want to harm, it's her."

The teen's reaction wasn't the reaction Lace expected. Instead of guilt or dread or anger, a deep resignation appeared at her aura. The little girls clung to Pansy.

Lace leaned forward. "What did you do to Hierarch Willow?"

Pansy clenched her fists. "What will happen to my family?"

Scad.

That was basically an admission of guilt. Oh gods, what had that girl done? How could she split and soil her soul, flood it with the misery of murder? No matter how angry or sinned against, that sacrifice of soul splitting was not worth it.

And dammit, she was the last person Lace wanted to find as the murderer. She was hoping it'd turn out to be one of King James' assassins, not a scared little girl.

"If you turn yourself in to us peacefully, we'll protect your family," Delia said.

Pansy took a deep breath. A gust of cold wind blew across the wall and shook the flowers and leaves. "I killed Hierarch Willow with her own knife."

Lace wished with all her heart that her aura split at the lie—but it didn't. She believed she was telling the truth.

The littlest girl started crying.

"But the knife didn't kill the Hierarch," Delia said. "Do you mean you strangled the Hierarch to death?"

Pansy fell to her knees, confused and weak. Her shoulders slumped and she spoke in a dull voice. "That woman stole my whole world. I snuck into the mansion . . . I didn't even go to kill her, I swear. But—I-I-I just had to tell her that-what she had done—I don't know. But then I saw her home.

She took a deep breath. "It's so stupid, they have a room just for a bath. I hear they have a room just for butterflies, too. Yeah . . . some people sleep in the streets but at least those butterflies have homes? So stupid. It made me so mad I couldn't think, I lost myself and just needed to—to make it end. So I found her knife and . . . and I killed her there."

Lace winced. "You strangled her?"

Pansy shook her head. "She was resting in a chair, and the bathing room was steamy so I just grabbed the knife and killed her."

That proved it. Pansy didn't kill Hierarch Willow; she arrived after the woman was already dead. Gods, there were a lot of people after her that night.

Chapter Twenty-Eight
Little Powers

The ropes binding Lace turned into pasta and fell off her hands. She stood, rubbing her wrists.

The children gasped.

Pansy's hands glowed with magic. Lace clutched the air's aura around her and moved her into the air—Pansy yelped in surprise.

"We will turn you into newt jelly if you don't behave," Delia said.

Lace lowered her gently down.

The twins ran and clutched Pansy. "Are you going to hang her?" they asked in terror.

"No one's getting hung," Delia said firmly as she stood up. "But we need to investigate your sister's story." She looked Pansy deep in the eye. "Because of your actions, the consequences are very dire for the entire town. You must come with us."

"You're all in grave danger," Violet said. "Go inside and don't come out for anything, even if the town is on fire."

Lace didn't know if that was exactly the best advice, seeing as the children could get trapped in a burning house, but she didn't argue with Violet. They'd come back later to save the children before they left Seagrove.

They had to.

"Go," Pansy told the children. "Now." She tried peeling them off her.

They clung to her even tighter. The sky grew darker and oppressive and the wind shook the leaves in the trees until they rustled. "If you have to go, we'll go with you," the littlest said.

"No!" Pansy wrenched away from them.

An aura approached outside the gate and it looked dangerous. She recognized it as someone from the fried cheese store, but she couldn't tell who it was. With the side of her mouth she clicked at Delia, then motioned with her eyes towards the door. Delia understood.

"Come with us," Violet said gently as she approached Pansy. "We won't hurt you."

"You aren't going to take her!" The littlest girl screamed, clenched her eyes, and then a force of magic exploded outwards.

The ground trembled and earth shot up. Everything was clouded with dust and white pebbles. A dirt clod smacked Lace in the face and she cried out, holding her eye.

That little girl could control *earth*.

Violet dove behind a tree. Lace flew up to escape the crumbling dirt below them, grabbing Delia's aura as she went. Delia shouted in surprised as she was lifted into the air. A cloud of dust rose around them.

The whole garden was torn up—bushes capsized and flowers uprooted.

Lace landed them on the other side of Pansy—between her and the gate—just as the aura came through.

It was the young man with the hot head. When he saw that they'd surrounded Pansy and the kids, he drew his sword. "Stay away from them!"

Delia instantly turned his sword into a long-stemmed sunflower. "Let's go." She grabbed Pansy's arm.

"No!" Lace cried.

In that moment, the man ran and tackled Delia. Pansy flared with yellow magic and then disappeared.

Violet controlled a tree branch hanging over the entryway, and wrapped it around the young man's middle and pushed him against the wall, trapping him with the branches. He struggled against the immovable wood. Lace grabbed the air around Delia and helped her back up.

Swirls of wind shot from the sky and lightning arced across the gray clouds.

The little boy screamed, and the littlest girl covered her ears with her hand, face wrinkled in distress, and shouted in fear. It was the loudest sound Lace had ever heard; it was almost otherworldly. Chills went down Lace's spine and bumps erupted on her arm.

Loud cracking sounded and the wall behind Lace shattered. Flying debris hurtled towards her. Hazy projectiles. Stones flew everywhere. Heavy. Dangerous.

Lace spread her arms and shielded Delia and Violet's bodies with her own, pushing them down to the ground. She braced for the attack.

Delia's magic flared red. A sea of glistening bubbles surrounded them. Delia had transformed the attack just in time.

Something smashed into Lace's temple and her head exploded in pain.

Then everything went black.

Chapter Twenty-Nine
Rest

She felt herself being pulled, yanked, roughly hauled across the stone. Painful pressure built in her head and she couldn't move. What was going on? Her memories were cloudy.

Warm liquid—blood maybe—poured down her neck. Garbled voices rose on top of her.

They stopped and someone urgently called her name, slapping her gently on the cheek at the same time. Lace startled awake, and feeling flooded through her. She sat up, then winced. The pounding in her head was unbearable.

Violet and Delia leaned over her. Delia still had her arm—she'd been dragging her. The street looked like there'd been a war there. Rubble blocked the road, dirt coated everything, and the garden wall had a huge hole in it.

"Pansy . . ." Lace struggled to get up but Violet pressed her shoulder, keeping her down.

"Escaped," Violet said. "Oh scad, Lace, you're bleeding everywhere!"

Blood trickled down her cheek and dripped off her chin, soaking into the ground. Violet quickly tore off the end of her waist-scarf and wrapped it around Lace's head, pressing the wound to stop the blood flow.

"Don't take too much off your scarf," Delia said. "There's precious little material as it is."

A few people gathered at the end of the road, staring at the destruction. Lace's hands were trembling, though it wasn't from nerves as much as it was from the pain.

"How are you?" Violet asked in concern.

Lace gingerly touched her bleeding head. "I feel as if my head was smashed with a huge rock."

"I'm so sorry." Delia's voice was heavy with regret. "You pulled us away just in time and I thought I'd transformed everything, but—"

"Don't worry." Lace touched Delia's arm, eyes closed. "It's nothin' important . . . just my head." She gave a weak smile.

"Where's Cannon when you need him?" Violet said.

The ground swam before Lace's eyes and she went limp.

Delia clutched Lace tightly, lowering her carefully to the

ground. Her eyes were wide in awe and concern. Sweaty curls framed her face and a thin layer of dust settled over her dress and skin.

Delia handed Violet her handkerchief and pressed it to the wound on the back of Lace's neck. She hissed in pain. It stung and throbbed when touched.

"We're going to get you back to the Hierarch's . . ."

Delia's voice faded away.

***

Lace woke.

There was a cool cloth over her forehead.

She was in an empty room, encased in softness.

The bed was plush, the sheets were cool silk. Her jacket and shoes were off, laying on the side of the bed, and the thin white shirt untucked from her pants.

The sky outside the window was dark.

How had she gotten here? Where was everybody?

Everything hurt—from the bruises on her face to the sore muscles in her legs. Even breathing hurt. Even staying still hurt.

Suddenly the door opened and a familiar aura approached.

"You're awake," Raj said. As soon as he closed the door, his whole complexion changed. The wall over his soul melted and his green eyes turned soft and compassionate. He viewed her with such vulnerability that she instantly mirrored it.

"I've still got four appendages so there's nothing to worry about, considering." She struggled to get up but he rushed forward and placed a hand on her shoulder.

"Don't get up." He sat on the bed. "Cannon says you're to rest for at least an hour. He healed you but you lost so much blood."

"An hour? How did I—last thing I knew I was in town."

"Delia commandeered a cart for you, and Violet drove it here. Delia carried you with her own two arms . . . she's stronger than she looks."

"Wow," Lace breathed. "They took good care of me."

"Cannon was replenished enough to heal you completely."

Lace touched her throbbing head and found the blood wiped clean.

"I cleaned the wounds," he said softly.

She looked deeply at him, imagining him cleaning her face. In the dim light his features were softened. The sharpness of his cheekbones was balanced by the gentle curve of his lips. She saw in his aura he felt safe.

For some reason, she had to say it. "I feel safe now."

"I wondered if I might—if I may . . . may I—?" he began, then stopped, embarrassed. He cleared his throat. "As a monk I was trained in the art of massage. By rubbing certain pressure points I can alleviate pain and help your body heal and—"

Lace interrupted, "Yes, yes, please yes. You had me at massage. Do whatever you want to me." She rolled onto her stomach and rested her head in her hands.

His reach was tentative. At first his hand hovered over her back, as if not knowing when to start, his breathing shallow. When his fingers touched her and pressed into her stiff muscles, she gave such a deep sigh and melted into the bed even more.

He rubbed with long motions, lightly caressing her skin. Warmth spread through the thin fabric of her shirt.

"Gods, that feels amazing," she whispered. His aura flared in pleasure.

With even movements Raj started gently rubbing key spots on her back. Upper shoulder, middle of the back, and right above her kidneys. Over and over again he'd press the same spots until one time he laid his palms flat on the very middle of her back and it was as if her soul left her body.

She felt no more pain.

The terrible feelings in her muscles were gone and she felt relief. And though she knew it wouldn't last, she savored the rush of energy.

His hands were strong and gentle, practiced. Yet she felt

them on her in a way that was intensely personal. She relaxed into the pleasure and savored it with every fiber of her being.

With his fingertips he thread through her hair and massaged her head. A soft moan escaped her lips, then she laughed.

"What?" he said.

"I'm just—" she stopped, unsure why she laughed. "I just feel so good."

She heard his lips part in a smile. At the thought of his smile her stomach melted and her heart burned.

He lightly turned her onto her back. A tendril of hair fell in her eyes and he brushed it back. Surrounding them, their auras glowed and flickered, relaxed yet intense at the same time, a focused peace. And wow, they were the exact same color. She sat up in bed, her heart in her eyes. "Raj," she said and put her hand on his shoulder, pulling him towards her.

His lips were full and parted—his breath as raspy as hers. Veins grew in his arms and neck, displaying his ardor. He swallowed and his eyes trailed down her face.

As natural as anything that she'd ever done, she slipped her arm around his neck and drew him to her. She had to feed this need in her, the longing to connect as their auras had.

"No," he said in anguish and then wrenched away. He stumbled off the bed and gripped his hair, pacing back and forth. The auras were torn apart. His turned green with turmoil and hers washed out with anger.

All the pain came rushing back, and it felt even worse than before. Every cell in her body ached. She felt old and worn, like she'd been stretched in a way she was never supposed to.

"Why?" she asked, and she wished her voice was stronger but it trembled. He shot a pained look at her, then glanced away, as if unable to bear the sight.

"Why?" she asked, stronger this time.

He strode to the bed and leaned forward, his green eyes earnest and honest. "I cannot need this."

The hurt was biting at her soul but she tried to keep it away, she tried to face him with honesty. "What do you mean?"

"You are just—just—" he sputtered, unable to phrase what he needed to. "You are just more than I ever thought possible. And with you came all the feelings of life and spirit and longing that I've put away my whole life. You can see everything. Can't *you* see that? How much you mean to me?"

The light reflected off his skin, causing a glow.

"But at the same time, I joined an academy and a rebellion and so much depends on us. And we've all sworn to the life of a traitor and—" here his voice shook, "it's very, very dangerous. Both lives can't happen at once."

"Why not?" she whispered. The room suddenly felt hot. Couldn't there be happiness and sorrow in the same life? In the same moment? Tears often cleansed the soul so joy could be felt stronger.

But at the same time, she felt the truth in his words. How could she attack King James if every moment she was terrified of the thought of Raj being captured and tortured and killed? Their physical separation could mean the difference between a clear head and a stupid, panicked error.

What he couldn't see was the extent to which their auras were already mixing together. Their lives were woven in. And that was exactly what Bahir had ordered them to do.

"So no kissing?" she said in a quiet voice.

He turned his back to her and she saw the overwhelming battle taking place in his mind. "If I could . . ." he began. If he could, he would get as close as humanly possible, he would be in her.

But he was strong enough to stop himself.

Well, she wasn't strong enough to stop.

Curling her legs up under her, she stood on the bed. At the rustle of sheets, Raj turned. In one leap, she jumped on him, wrapping her arms around his shoulders and legs around his hips. He caught her around the waist, pulling her tight. He was solid and strong, her soft flesh molded to his. Leaning in, their lips met.

His tongue parted her teeth, caressing her mouth. They shared a breath. Her chest trembled and he gripped her closer. The kiss was fierce, needed—like a gasp of breath after being underwater. She slid her fingers across the back of his neck and he pressed her thighs into him.

It was a kiss she felt all the way to her toes. Longing and joy erupted in her, and she felt as if her entire being were replenished.

The door burst open. Cannon charged through. "Oh gods!" he said, then jumped out and slammed the door. "Hey!" he shouted through the closed door. "Lace is supposed to be resting!"

Lace hid her face in Raj's shoulder and giggled in embarrassment. Raj still hadn't recovered his breath from the kiss. She searched his face, slowly pulling away their auras as if he was a fire and she couldn't get too close to the heat.

"Professor Bahir wants you!" Cannon called. "There's been another attack."

Lace's stomach dropped. She climbed off of Raj, who gently set her down. "Who?" she asked as she shouldered into her jacket.

"Sylvia."

Lace broke into a run.

Chapter Thirty
Falling Pieces

The door to the slave's quarters where they had put Sylvia was open. The small room was full of people.

Lace rushed in. Sylvia was in the bed, limp as a rag. Her hair was wet with sweat and there was the smell of vomit in the room. Cannon took a cloth by the side of the bed and started dabbing her forehead and neck.

In the corner, Delia held a knife to Maeve's throat. It pressed on his Adam's apple so that every time he swallowed it cut him. His aura reeked of bitterness and he was glaring at Delia, only she took about as much notice of him as if he were a gecko on the wall.

So *he* had the gall to attack Sylvia! How'd he get past the lock?

The young girl was in the corner of the room. Violet and

Professor Bahir leaned over an empty glass, bread, and cheese on a plate, examining it closely.

"What happened?" Lace asked. "Is Sylvia . . ." She faded off, not wanting to even consider that Sylvia might be dead.

Professor Bahir glanced at her. "Ah, good. You're here. Now we can question Maeve. We have very little time. The Centurions will be here soon."

Delia brought the knife even closer to his neck.

"What did he do?" Lace asked, worried.

"I obeyed my master," Maeve lashed out. Delia shoved him back with the palm of her hand, then steadied the knife on his pulsing jugular.

"What happened?" Raj repeated her question.

"The food Delia brought for Sylvia was poisoned with rockweed." Violet shuddered. "If Delia hadn't stayed to talk with Sylvia, she wouldn't have been there when the poison took effect."

"You saved Sylvia," Cannon said over his shoulder with a smile.

"No, *you* saved Sylvia," Delia said. "The discovery would've been as useless as a fan in a windstorm if there was no way to heal her."

Violet sniffed and sniffed, nearing Maeve, as if searching for something. "I can smell the rockweed still on him. He's definitely handled the powder in the past few hours."

"I needed to save us," Maeve said. "If she's dead then perhaps King James will—"

"Forget it happened?" Delia interrupted with a voice full of scorn. "No, you fool. He will mete out the murderer's punishment on all of you."

"What will happen to Sylvia?" Lace asked. She wiped her forehead. The room was getting hot from all the bodies.

"She'll be fine," Cannon said, taking off his hat and fanning his face with it. "The rockweed is out of her system, she's just sleeping."

"You've doomed us all!" Maeve said in anguish. "King James will destroy everything."

Professor Bahir's eyes saddened. "That has already happened, no way to waylay it. Murder is no way out, Maeve. It never is. So Stim told you to kill her?"

Maeve's face paled so that his freckles stood out. He pressed his lips together and his aura settled into a hazy gray cloud. Bahir looked at Lace. "What's his aura saying?"

"Nothing," Lace said. "But I remember Hierarch Stim had said he was going to execute Sylvia at noon. This could be on his orders. His last, desperate act to save the town."

Maeve's aura flared and Lace raised her eyebrows and nodded. "Yes. It's on Stim's orders."

"An act of revenge," Violet said.

"Or," Delia said in a loud tone. "A cover up."

"What do you mean?" Professor Bahir's sharp eyes pierced hers.

Delia addressed them all, looking from one face to the next. "When we found the Kinkade family, the eldest said Willow was sleeping on the bathing chair and she plunged the knife in her—but I think Willow had already been strangled and was arranged in that position."

"Right. The knife was stuck in a dead body," Cannon said.

Delia's eyes lit. "So what if Stim killed his wife, then left her there knowing that he could blame Sylvia for the murder?"

Professor Bahir folded his arms over his chest and leaned back against the table, his wrinkly face thoughtful.

Lace felt like that was the closest anyone had come so far . . . but it just didn't snap right in place. Her mind kept turning the same thoughts over and over again—the button, the baby, the bathing time—and she was on the cusp of understanding something important and all she had to do was put the pieces together, but they were still scattered at her feet.

"That's why he moved her," said a small voice from the corner.

Everyone looked, surprised, to find the young girl frowning fiercely. She grasped fistfuls of her apron in her hand, as if barely controlling herself. "Master asked Sylvia to nanny the babe last night instead of me. To get her out of the way."

Everything was becoming clearer. "That way Hierarch Willow would be alone in the morning," Raj said.

Though some of the puzzle pieces pointed to Stim, not all of them did. Lace buttoned and unbuttoned the top of her jacket as she sifted all the information in her mind. "What I don't understand is how Stim hid his darkness from me—I should have seen the murder in his aura."

"You could be wrong," Delia suggested in the same moment that Cannon stood up from the bedside and said, "But why? Why would he do it?"

Professor Bahir spoke for the first time. "He thinks he's doing the right thing. Perhaps he found out that Willow was a part of the rebellion and wanted to protect his son and family from her inevitable fate."

No, Lace did not think that was it. Stim could not have been lying when he discovered Willow was still working with Bahir. No one was that good at deceit.

"After all, I believe I'm doing good even though I'm leading all my trusting students into dire danger and overwhelming odds," he said. "Scad, it is almost noon. We must hurry. Arif gave us some extra time, but not much. I don't want One Eye to be alone if the Centurions teleport across the magnetic road."

"Is he safe?" Violet asked, alarmed.

"For now," Bahir said. "Even without Arif's storm they couldn't have made it here this fast. But we have to leave in the next twenty minutes or we may be in for a bloody battle. I need to collect any ties Willow had with me and the rebellion, but most importantly we need to find the murderer."

Delia ignored that. "How can we prove it?" she asked.

The button. The button! Oh gods, she knew what happened!

Lace's eyes suddenly locked to Violet. "I know!" She fairly jumped on her toes and flew to her, grasping her arm. "And you can prove it. But first . . ." she turned to the young girl. "Go get Jon's night clothes and meet us in the library."

Chapter Thirty-One

The Button
and the Scent

Back in the library, the family had started a fire in the heavy, pink-brick fireplace. Flames crackled and sparks popped and flew up the chimney. The stained glass window glowed with light, flickering bits of color onto the floor.

Mary and the child were asleep on the couch—their chests rose and fell evenly, their faces were blank and peaceful in rest, so far away from all the grief and death around them.

Jon was at the desk, writing something. When they came in he quickly turned the paper over and stood.

Stim was staring into space, his head in his hand. Before him sat a stack of letters—she noticed they were the emancipation papers. He straightened, then stood as they approached. They formed a half circle around the men.

Cannon had stayed back to care for Sylvia, and Professor Bahir had locked Maeve in another room.

Everyone looked to her.

This was it. Lace swallowed. It changed history to accuse people of something as monumental as murder—it'd forever change their aura, like it had Sylvia's—and it might start something rolling that could never be stopped.

She dearly wished she wasn't the one to have to do it.

Taking a deep breath, she set her jaw. It was their mission. And at the thought of Hierarch Willow's corpse and the blame going to Sylvia, Lace gathered the courage to bring this accusation into being.

Lace whispered something in Violet's ear. She first looked surprised, then understanding lit her features.

Violet padded over to the mother and child. The necklaces jangled as she walked. Her face softened as she looked at their still figures, then she leaned over, holding her necklaces so they stayed in place, then sniffed their breath.

"What are you—" Jon began, then stopped when Violet lithely walked to him and grabbed his wrist and took a long sniff of his hand. He jerked it out of her grip, but not before she turned to Lace and gave a deep bow.

Lace grew somber.

Then there was a knock on the door, and the young girl entered holding a white robe.

"What the hell?" Jon cried, stiffening. "What is she doing with that?" The black void in his soul, the tear, was widening and swirling—his aura surrounded in fear. Things were unraveling.

The girl walked up to Lace and gave it to her. Then she went to the couch and sat beside the sleeping child, putting her arm around the back of the couch in a protective gesture.

Lace held up the robe and snapped out the wrinkles.

"Oh," Delia said, her face fallen.

Lining the front of the robe were bone buttons. Professor Bahir took out the button Arif had found from his pocket and held it out. It was a perfect match.

"You drugged your wife with rockweed," Lace said, suddenly overcome with anger. "You arranged Willow to be alone in the bathing room. You strangled her there, a button falling off your robe during the struggle." She took a step towards him. "Then you let Sylvia take the blame."

At each one of her accusations, Jon became more and more angry. His face reddened and veins popped up on his neck and arms. "How dare you accuse me!" he shouted. "I will not be spoken to by a damned brownie!"

Before Lace could even react Delia slapped him across the face. "Don't call her brownie," she said fiercely. "Don't call *anyone* brownie."

Lace's heart swelled at the defense. Jon shriveled at

Delia's ferocity.

"But Jon didn't do it," Stim said, his eyes wide in shock, his voice trembling. It was as if speaking the words would make them true. "It was Sylvia. She was caught with the knife."

Professor Bahir shook his head. "The knife didn't kill your wife. She was strangled by a towel. Then a child from town, one of the Kinkade's daughters, snuck in and stabbed Willow. Sylvia confessed to the murder so she could protect the children."

Stim's eyes darkened with turmoil. "There you go, it was the villagers. I knew they always hated her. The poor are never satisfied with their lot and blame those in power."

Jon leaned towards the couch and his family. "I don't know why my button was in the pool or why my wife was drugged but I was never in the bathing room. Never even near Willow. Now let us go."

"That's a big lie," Lace said calmly. "Your aura just about tore in half."

Jon seemed to wither before their eyes. The deepness of his trouble must be starting to sink in. Lace hated that he hadn't seen trouble at the murder—only at being caught. And though Lace could see through him clearly, he still didn't admit anything.

"Why did you do it?" Delia nearly shouted.

"She ruined my life," he said. "I had every right to kill her, but I didn't—"

Professor Bahir's aura grew so full of rage that he turned away and covered his mouth with his hand, taking even breaths.

"Ruined your life?" Stim said. "What the hell do you mean?"

Jon came within an inch of his father's face, steaming with intensity. "She's the one who got me cut from the university. And you let it happen!"

He sounded just like a petulant child, not an intellectual leader.

"To save your life," Stim yelled, and the two sleepers on the couch woke up. The little girl cried out. But the two men were so heated they didn't even notice. "King James would have wiped you out first if something happened in Seagrove. And now it has. And we'll be tortured and killed, unless we migrate to another country."

The child's sleepy cries rose until the whole room resounded with them. Mary patted her back and kissed her chubby cheeks, trying to soothe her. The wails only grew louder.

"You don't know what you've done, killing Willow," Delia said. "You've destroyed the only protection you ever had."

"If you had only asked her you would have known!" Stim's voice broke. His face scrunched up in agony. "But you never ask. You always think you know." Then he collapsed in the chair with his hands over his face. His shoulders shook with sobs.

Jon licked his lips and looked around, his aura flaring with complicated, conflicting emotions. "I-I-I didn't want that," he said slowly. His aura's black crack widened and Lace winced to see the destruction.

Every lie hurt one's soul, but some lies scarred for all eternity. This lie was one of those.

Lace watched in compassion as his aura kept splitting, changing his identity and emotions so they grew colder and harder than ever. "May the gods have mercy on your cracked soul," Lace said. "Because King James won't."

Chapter Thirty-Two
Escape Ship

Lace ran down the hallway with a handful of papers. Sharp points of light washed over her as she sped past the windows' light. Her breath caught in her chest and she took steady breaths, drawing air from her nose like Da had taught her to.

She slowed and stutter stepped as she rounded the corner then burst into the main hallway. Lining the pristine wall were the slaves. Sweat coated their skin and soaked their clothes. It looked like they were drowning in the murky heat.

Time to make them feel a lot better.

Violet had been sent to find the mage children and bring them to safety, Lace had been sent to free the slaves. And Arif had been sent to hire a boat to take them away.

Going first to the double doors, she swung them open.

Instantly a cool wind flooded through. She heard relieved sighs erupt behind her. The storm clouds rolled and rollicked in the sky, black and blue, with a fierce lightning and thunder show about a mile off.

Though Arif wasn't doing his magic anymore, the storm was still going strong.

Holding up the papers, she said crisply. "Here are your emancipation papers. Hierarch Stim has freed you."

No one moved. Distrust flared in their auras, as if she were trying to trap them. The eldest shifted, frowned, and was about to say something then he held back.

"I'll read your name," Lace said. "Then come and receive your papers. There's a carriage waiting to take you to a boat and carry you across the border. But we have to—"

The white haired man interrupted, "Let me see it!"

Lace started thumbing through the papers. "What's your name?"

"They called me Peter," he said.

She found his name and held it out. With trepidation, as if even the hope of it was too much to bear, he walked forward and slowly took it out of her hand.

His eyes scanned every word of it. For a minute all he did was gaze at it and swallow a few times, his eyes reddening. He swallowed. "Why are you doing this?"

Lace looked down, so he couldn't read her. Speaking

quietly, she said, "There are those who work for the good, even from bad places." She felt him studying her.

Then he turned and held the paper high in the air. "It's real!" he whooped. And a murmur of unbelief and excitement went through them. "We can't be accused of being a runaway. It'll get us to the border, all right!"

They started crowding around her, asking questions and accepting their papers. Most of them had been kidnapped from their home country, but one young girl said it was the first freedom she'd ever tasted.

Lace seemed to get something in her eye when she handed the papers away.

***

Everyone met back in the slave quarters where Sylvia and Cannon were. On their way, Bahir announced that he'd found all the hidden material Willow had left that related to their rebellion—a few paper books, and a ring. He then gave them to Delia for safekeeping. She slipped the ring on her finger.

"You're a rebel now," Lace said.

"My mother would not approve," she said with a pert smile. "Which means it's definitely the right thing to do."

When they got back in the simple room, Cannon had helped Sylvia gather her things. Her strength had returned, though she was groggy, and blinked slowly, as if not understanding what was going on. That much rockweed would certainly put her head in the clouds.

"You're free to go—" Professor Bahir started.

"Free?" Sylvia interrupted.

Lace smiled. "Free." She handed her the paper.

The woman perused it, frowning, her lips slightly moving as she read. She bit her lip and looked from Bahir to the paper, as if trying to find a loophole but unable to. "I'm my own again?" There was awe in her voice.

"You've always been your own," Raj said.

"Raj was born a slave and I lived as a slave for most my life, we know what it's like," Violet said. Her face reddened and she rubbed her nose. She cleared her throat then said in a low voice, "I'm so glad you're free."

"I'm sure we could find a new home here for her somewhere if she needs it," Delia said. "In case she doesn't want to leave Dram."

"What?" Lace said. Her heartbeat slowed and her mouth hung open. As if the masters were taking slaves in because they needed a place to stay? Even Raj's look showed rare emotion.

"She'll go back to her country," Raj said fiercely.

"She's been kidnapped," Lace snapped.

"WHAT?" Delia nearly shouted. "Who kidnapped her?"

Her aura was bright with confusion and surprise—she'd

fallen into revealing more of her ignorance, and her aghast expression was acute. She hugged herself, shrinking back a step.

Lace put a hand on Sylvia's arm. "What did you do in Vingiz before this hell?"

Sylvia smiled slowly, meeting Lace's eyes. "I was a doctor. The skill had been passed down for generations. I made medicine and helped birth babies and set bones and kept my town from too much harm." Then her face grew stony. "I was riding with my daughters when the Dram soldiers—"

Cannon cut in, alarmed. "You mean merchants?"

"No," Sylvia said. "Soldiers."

Cannon swallowed and exchanged a look with Delia. "King James always told the Hierarchs that he'd never take the slave trade away from the merchants."

Raj ruffled his hair with his hand. "So King James is a liar. We already knew that."

"They sold us straight to Stim," Sylvia continued. "And when they needed money, they-they-they took my babies away from me." She stopped, unable to continue. Everyone stilled, silent. It was intolerable.

Though Lace could never think well of her, she realized that Willow was just doing what she thought right. Selling her slaves for the sake of saving the people in her village.

Using that money to pay the war tax and keep everyone out of it was good—but at a deplorable cost.

"Do you know where they are?" Lace asked.

Sylvia nodded. "They were sold to King James' quarries. In the north."

Delia trembled and took Cannon's arm, as if looking for comfort. Her eyes welled with tears and her bottom lip trembled. She looked so miserable, so unsure of herself, it was as if she'd become another person.

If ignorance was bliss, then knowledge was pain.

But it was also light. And from now on, Lace hoped Delia would start living in it. Lace knew she would. She'd learned and changed so much already, even just within the past day, that Lace felt a new confidence in the former queen of Dram.

Sylvia turned to Professor Bahir. "You know, Willow talked about you."

"Oh?" Bahir's expression was tentative, as if he didn't want to hear what came next.

"She said you were her favorite person to talk to. She said that you bring up the most trivial historical facts and it always made her laugh, that you have the worst fashion sense . . . she said that you had no tolerance for alcohol and can get stone cold drunk from the first glass of wine—"

Lace listened in fascination at the intimate picture that

was being told.

Sylvia went on, "And she said that the happiest time in her life was when you both completed your studies at that cottage . . . um, what was it? Boniface?"

"Bonnick," Bahir said softly. "The cottage in Bonnick."

The grief in his aura was palpable, as if it sucked all the air to him.

Willow went on. "And she said you can grill the best spicy shrimp . . ."

"And she could bake the best herbed bread," Bahir said.

"She can bake?" Sylvia raised her eyebrows.

"Oh, yes," Bahir said. "She loved kneading the warm dough, taking all day to craft the food . . . I expect being a Hierarch changed that." He swallowed.

"She probably didn't change as much as you think," Sylvia said. "Everyone's just got to hold on to what they love while they can."

They were all still, eyes glazed in thought, thinking of all that had been lost.

And all there was to lose.

***

Arif had the boat rented and ready. The people had packed, the former slaves had been paid their relinquished wages in the form of Willow's gold plates, the Kinkades and the Hierarch's family were pale and scared and sad.

Streams of villagers were loading their things onto ships and taking off, even in the midst of the storm. They'd get carried away by the wind and skirt the coast—probably end up in Cape Bluefish, a bustling seaport in a country neighboring Zoto. From there they could find homes and start a new life.

Lace noticed a few of them had grape vines packed into cans—that made her smile. She wouldn't object to Seagrove's delicious wine being made so close to Zoto.

Jon was still locked in the Hierarch's mansion. Trapped. Surrounded by his precious books, worth more to him than his stepmother's life. He'd be the only one in the house to greet the Centurions when they arrived.

While Professor Bahir gave instructions to the ship's captain and the rest of the students helped the people up the gangplank, Delia held Lace back.

She looked down, unsure of what to say. They just stood there for a moment as the gulls called and swooped over them and the bugs droned in the grass.

"I just wanted to say that I'm learning a lot. From everybody." She looked Lace in the eye. "From you. I've always thought I was open minded but I realize now I was seeing everything from my gilded cage."

Lace tensed, not really knowing how to reassure her without spouting platitudes. So she kept quiet.

"And I promise you that when I become Queen of Dram I shall set all the slaves free and outlaw slavery forever." Her aura flared with earnestness. "Not only that, but I shall reimburse every slave a fair wage—" she stuttered. "It's-it's no recompense for what they've suffered, but at least it will give them something to travel back home with and start their life again."

Lace's heart warmed to hear it. At least Delia was quick to put her newfound belief into action. "Well then." Lace folded her arms across her chest. A gust of wind rushed between them. "If you do that then I promise, when I am Queen of Zoto, that I will not go to war with you to free the slaves."

Delia smiled, her pearly teeth flashing. She stuck out her hand. "It's a pact, then."

Lace shook her hand. "A pact."

And some of the icy distrust she felt towards Delia thawed at that touch. Perhaps, if they kept working together, they might be good allies. Possibly even friends.

A good ally was priceless during this time of war.

They watched that boat take off. Several other boats had filled with villagers.

Suddenly, a *boom* erupted to the west. It was so loud that the sand shook and the vibrations jarred her bones. Everyone turned. It was not thunder, nor did it come from the town.

It was beyond. Arif's dark clouds still twisted and twirled in the sky, the storm like a great wall separating them from the capitol.

But something had gotten through.

"What was that?" Lace asked, her heart racing. She feared she knew the answer but still dreaded it.

"The Centurions are close," Professor Bahir said. His magic was almost completely replenished—which meant he could easily make them a portal back to Moth Valley.

But that meant . . .

"One Eye needs help!" Lace leapt into the air, caught the aura, and shot towards the heart of the storm.

Chapter Thirty-Three
Starting

"Wait!" Raj yelled at her.

"Stop!" Professor Bahir ordered.

She turned in midair, hovering. The wind licked her neck. Cool. Unstable. The void around her cradled her body in its pocket. The infinite sea spread out before her, dotted with the retreating ships.

"We can't abandon One Eye to face the Centurions alone," she said loudly enough for her voice to carry.

"What do you mean, we?" Violet said. "You mean *you*? Don't just leave us."

But . . . what else was there to do? She was the only one who could fly. And the Centurions must be close. One Eye shouldn't face them alone.

"You have to carry us there." Professor Bahir's wrinkled

face was tranquil. He'd had a peace around him since the talk with Sylvia.

"What?" She was so startled she tripped in the aura and fell a ways before catching herself. "I can't do that! I can only carry Raj."

"We have no time for that," Professor Bahir said. "I know you are strong enough. The battle is with your mind."

Of course the battle was with her mind! She didn't know how to do it. How could she keep track of so much aura? With Raj it was easy, because their auras had been knit together. But she couldn't knit everyone's aura together. And if she failed again . . . it would be One Eye's life at stake.

"And remember," Delia said. "Remember what I taught you about it?"

Ah, that's right.

Rain started falling in stinging drops. The sound of the waves seemed to swell, as if it were reaching up to meet the water in the sky.

If she could make pockets of air for the team, then she could carry all of them. No need to weave her aura with theirs—only control the air around them.

Could she do it?

"Please," Violet begged. "We need you to take us. Or it may be too late." Her heart was in her eyes—desperately worried about One Eye.

Lace landed on the ground so hard it made her stumble. She looked from face to face, sizing their auras and how much it would take to hold them all—Raj was looking at her with worry in his black eyes. Her heart sped, thudding in her ear. She didn't even know where to start.

Chapter Thirty-Four
Pockets

"Lace," Professor Bahir said. "We have to hurry."

"Let's go, Lace," Cannon said with an encouraging smile. "You were able to carry that huge iron block back at the air temple—you'll be able to carry us. You can do it!"

She lifted herself off the ground just as Raj made his way for her with a determined expression. "Lift me first," he said.

With a flick of her wrist she lifted him into the air. He lurched forward and she reached up and grabbed his chest. Then he twirled around and she caught him, breathless, her hands hovering around his neck.

"Enough of that!" Arif said. "We've got a battle to fight."

"No," Cannon said, alarmed. "Not fight!"

"He's right," Professor Bahir said. "We have a battle to flee from. You are not ready to fight the Centurions. Not yet.

Lace, are you ready to carry us?"

She had to be.

She wiped the rain off her face and undid the buttons on her jacket. Raj floated right beside her.

"Carry six pockets," Delia called up to her.

"Six pockets," Lace repeated softly, then imagined them in her mind. She formed a cocoon with the air, then connected it with each person's aura. Arif, lithe and colorful. Violet, sweet and wild. Delia, proud and capable. Bahir, wise and fluid. Cannon, kind and smart. They all came into her mind and gathered there and she protected each one by air and then closing her eyes, lifted them. She raked her fingers up, and it was as if a great weight were hanging on the tips of each fingernail.

It drained her magic quickly as she concentrated on each person and each pocket, lifting, lifting . . . she peeked one eye open.

They were still on the ground.

Dammit!

"Just pockets," Delia said again. "Just make pockets."

Lace took a deep breath. So all she had to do was carry them as if they were an object with no soul—like the box?

Rain pelted the sand, creating craters in it.

Again, she closed her eyes. This time she didn't picture anyone, only the air's aura. She arranged them over each person in the group. With everything in her she wanted to connect to the auras of each person, but she held back.

Delia had been willing to learn from Lace, so she was willing to learn from her.

Not really believing it'd work, Lace easily lifted up the air pockets. They were as light as anything, with no strain.

The group shot into the air.

"Whoa!" she shouted. Leveling her hand, she slowed them down and spread them out so they wouldn't hit each other.

Violet's hair lay straight back in the wind. They moved their arms in jerky movements, not able to adjust to the non-space of flying.

How could it be this easy? It really just felt as if she were carrying nothing but napkins in her hand. It was remarkable how the air's aura did all the work for her. She met eyes with Delia and mouthed, *Thank you.*

"Go, go, go!" Violet said.

Making sure she had all seven of the auras, she flew them straight into the air, then leveled off. Leaning forward, she focused on keeping the students free from the wind's grip. Gaining confidence, she gained speed, and they hurtled through the air as fast as she ever had before. Her eyes watered and she grit her teeth.

If only they could make it before the Centurions.

They raced past the docks, then crossed the village. Pastures and farms whizzed past.

She felt her magic starting to wane, for the wind grew stronger and it took more effort to keep the pockets of air in place. It wasn't as easy to keep all six of them up. At a sudden gust, Cannon was almost taken from her grasp. He jerked to the side, crying out. With a grunt, she pulled him back.

"Don't lose me!" he shouted.

Sweat poured down her back and her face wrinkled in effort. "You can do this," Raj said. "Almost there."

At the top of the hill were the ruins. Lightning flashed around them, outlining the tall columns in light. The wind was so strong it blew the grass. She swept the area with her gaze.

Her stomach dropped.

One Eye wasn't there.

With a final push, they reached the top. She stopped right in front of the gigantic stone gateway covered with intricate carvings. Carefully, slowly, she lowered and then dropped the pockets of air and hoped that each person could catch themselves.

Her muscles trembled. She leaned over, panting, trying to catch her breath. She felt like she had just climbed straight up a cliff.

The rain made the stones slippery. Cannon landed

perfectly. Professor Bahir was unsteady—Cannon reached out to help balance him. Violet landed in a graceful crouch, while Delia wobbled and then jerked her arms out to balance herself. Arif, who was used to rolling surfaces, drew his sword and burst into a run the moment he landed.

His aura was scared, but he didn't give a sign of it on his face.

Lace was the closest to the ruins. She drew her knife and ran through the archway, with Raj right behind her. He was as steady as the tide. Gingerly, she ran on her toes, so as not to slip on the wet rocks.

The only sound in the place was the rumble of thunder, the rushing of long grass, and the raindrops smacking the ground. It smelled of fragrant earth and crackling electricity.

They rounded the bend and stopped dead in their tracks.

A massacre lay before them.

Bodies were piled on top of the other, each with their throat cut. Blood soaked into the ground. One of the cuts was so deep the head barely hung on. Glazed eyes stared blankly. Fear froze her and made her blood run cold and the smell made her stomach clench.

It was the Centurion's assistants. "Who did this?" Lace asked, horrified.

"One Eye," Raj said.

Another gust of wind tore through and made her stumble forward. She stopped herself and looked up to see One Eye with his back to them.

He was sitting beside one of the columns, cross-legged with his sword across his lap. His shoulders were relaxed, his hands were open palmed on his knees, and he was soaked through. But his aura was red and crackling with rage. What was he doing?

Maybe he'd been attacked, and was wounded. She jogged towards him, and heard Violet and Raj's step right behind. She slowed before she reached him, and another chill went through her.

She took a slow step. "One Eye? Are you all right?"

He still didn't turn. But she smelled blood on him and saw it dripping from his sleeves.

Holding her knife in front of her, she slipped around him. His eye was opened wide. Blood streamed out of it. His mouth was crooked and paralyzed, his chest contracted in spasm as if he were trying to yell.

Lace cried out, recoiling. "A curse!" she screamed. "Professor! Come quick!"

Just as she said that a black cloud descended from the sky, spreading darkness. She sensed auras inside it. Something shot into her mind—a foreign thought—*kill yourself, kill yourself, kill yourself*—repeating like an infant's wail. She shuddered at the feeling and everything went cold.

Bahir shot a spell at One Eye's back.

One Eye jerked, then his face returned to normal and his eye returned to its warm brown.

"Run!" Raj yelled. "It's a trap!"

Chapter Thirty-Five
The Massacre

Lace was surrounded by a funnel of darkness. It whipped her hair and gnawed at her skin. Not even the columns could be seen, or the dead bodies. *Kill yourself. Kill yourself. Kill yourself.* Looking around, she saw each student writhing as if in pain.

A circle of figures descended, making a ring around them. Though the apprentices all looked so different, the Centurions were identical. They wore orange masks, with tusks and black, gaping eyes, and brown pants and a gray striped cloak. Their auras were swollen with powerful magic. It was like a nightmare.

All the while, the voice dug into her brain like a worm—*kill yourself, kill yourself, kill yourself.* She looked down to find her knife at her own wrist. She screamed and dropped it, then pressed her hands over her ears to make the voice stop.

Beside her, Raj fell to the ground. He gave a soul-searing groan, as if burdened by the most potent pain. It killed her to hear it. Then he shuddered and cried out, twisting in agony.

Another curse pierced her body like lightning. White-hot pain seared inside, setting her blood on fire. She collapsed, writhing, crushing her hands to her heart in a vain attempt to keep it from exploding. The pain attacked in wave after wave, as fire burned through her.

Lace heard her name but couldn't recognize what to do. Tears ran down her cheeks. Someone called her again. She hunched her shoulders and squinted through her lashes. There was Bahir. He was impervious to the curses, for a yellow ring of light, looking almost like water, flowed around him. He looked straight at her.

She leaned forward, staring at his lips. "Lace," he said. "Carry everyone through the portal." Though he spoke clearly, she could barely understand through the pain.

Kill yourself. Kill yourself. Kill yourself. Came through like a song, luring and beautiful.

Another wave of pain wracked her body and she curled in a little ball, trying to overcome it. "Gods, oh gods, please help . . ." she thought. "Gods, help me." How could she get out of this?

She looked up again. Bahir was holding up a finger. *One.* He paused. Then he held up another finger. *Two.*

He was about to make a portal. And she was supposed to fly them all through it.

This was it, the only way to survive. Without taking her eyes off of Bahir, she gripped her aura. Her. Aura. It was bright blue with red swimming through it, white in pain.

She struggled with her mind, numbed by pain, and envisioned seven pockets, placing them on everyone she saw.

Then another curse erupted on top of the others. She convulsed on her back, her hands curled up and legs sprawled out. Everything fled her mind, she was paralyzed.

Kill yourself.

Then one aura came through—it knit around her in gold and blue, brilliant and beautiful. Raj crawled on his elbows towards her, grimacing every time he moved. "Lace." He grit his teeth. "Lace." Reaching her, he placed his hand on the middle of her stomach.

Their auras knit together, clinging like magnets, so close she could barely breathe. It was like Bahir had said—they were more powerful together. All the pain disappeared. All her magic returned.

Instantly she grabbed the seven pockets and shoved them at Bahir. She couldn't see who was who. She couldn't even see the portal. She trusted in one thing: carry everybody to Bahir.

There was an explosion of lightning and thunder so deep it shuddered in her soul.

Screaming at the weight around her, she shoved her hands forward and shot everyone towards the gold light.

She was sucked into blackness.

Chapter Thirty-Six
Alone

There was carpet at her back. Hair in her eyes. Pressure on her chest. Smoke in her nose. With a groan, she shifted, taking stock of what was going on.

Raj lay on her chest. His eyes were closed, his body limp. His hair was in his face. She curled up and brushed the hair out of his face—then cradled his head in her lap.

Violet trembled on the rug beside her. One Eye had her in his arms. Dried blood streaked down his face, coming from his eye. He looked like death—pale and drawn.

They were back in Moth Valley in Bahir's study.

Lace was right next to the fire—and it was a smoky one, shooting sparks as if it were eating wet wood.

"Is everyone all right?" Delia said in a trembling voice.

Raj was still unconscious, but his chest rose and fell in

steady breaths. She gently stroked his cheek. He had saved her back there. Something strange and mysterious happened when they united auras—and their power was getting stronger every time it happened.

"My back," Arif said. There was a grisly scrape, as if by a wildcat, all the way down his jacket. Blood seeped through the fabric. He slowly stood up, wincing.

Professor Bahir had his head in his hands. His aura was dark and in turmoil, almost panicked. When she saw it, another wave of fright washed over her. What was wrong?

"No," Delia said suddenly.

Lace looked around. What was the matter?

"No!" Delia said again, voice mangled in panic.

Lace laid Raj's head down on the carpet gently and scooted out from under him. What was it? A sinking feeling overtook her. Her breath quavered.

"Gods, no!" Delia shouted in anguish.

Lace looked around and her bottom lip trembled. Oh God. "Cannon," she whispered. "Cannon!" She jumped to her feet. Seven. She'd made seven air pockets. In the frantic pain and fight, she'd forgotten the healer.

"We have to go back!" Her voice wrenched.

Professor Bahir set his chin and spoke as if each word pained him. "No. If we do we'll be massacred."

Violet started sobbing.

"We have to!" Lace said. "We can't just leave him!"

Professor Bahir stood abruptly. "We will never leave him. But we can't go back."

"Then what are we going to do?" Delia asked.

"We're going to rescue him."

THE END